GET MORE OF MY BOOKS FREE!

To say thank you for buying this book, I'd like to invite you to my exclusive *VIP Club*, and give you some of my books and short stories for FREE.

To join the club, head to adamcroft.net/vip-club and two free books will be sent to you straight away! And the best thing is it won't cost you a penny — ever.

Adam Croft

For more information, visit my website: adamcroft.net

BOOKS IN THIS SERIES

Exit Stage Left is the first book in the Kempston Hardwick series.

To find out more about this series and others, please head to adamcroft.net/list.

The bell clattered as he closed the door behind him, shutting the cold winter air out of the Freemason's Arms. Loosening his tight woollen scarf, he approached the bar and signalled for the barmaid's attention. He seemed not to be interested in the vivacious curves of the young woman's slender body and placed his order without emotion.

He took a sip of the cool, bitter liquid and placed the glass back on the bar, watching the marbled effect of deep red mingling with orange. He took a drinking straw from the box on the bar and plunged it into his glass, stabbing at the ice cubes as the vibrant colours became one.

'Excuse me,' he said to the man who had now taken the place of the young woman behind the bar. 'Is tonight's act still on?' He was well-spoken, his voice verging on the baritone with an accent which was difficult to detect. As he spoke, he gestured towards the poster which was taped to the wall next to the bar. The poster advertised that night's entertainment, a stage routine by Charlie Sparks, former staple of Saturday night television and now another washed-up has-been.

'I should hope so,' the landlord replied. 'Had to pay him in advance. Bloomin' cheek, if you ask me. Not even been on telly in years.'

'I don't watch much television,' the man said, matter-of-factly.

Before the landlord had a chance to reply, another man, dressed in limbo between smart and casual, threw his tuppence-worth into the ring. 'Couldn't miss him twenty years ago! Hardly needed to pick up a magazine and he was in it. Oh, how the mighty have fallen...'

'I don't read many magazines,' the man said.

'Blimey. Don't get out much, do you?' the smart-casual, casual-smart man said.

'On the contrary. I'm out too much to take notice of such things.'

The smart-casual, casual-smart man did not quite know how to respond. In his half-professional, half-social style, he thrust out a hand. 'Ellis Flint.'

'Kempston Hardwick.'

'Pleasure to meet you.'

'Indeed.'

Ellis Flint, again unsure how to react, chose instead to speak to the landlord. 'Is he back there already, then?'

'Who?'

'Charlie Sparks! Is he already here?'

The landlord's tea-towelled grip on the pint glass tightened as his cleaning action got audibly squeakier. 'Yes. Backstage as we speak, drinking copious amounts of free booze and knackering my profit margins.'

'Surely he'll draw a big crowd though, eh?' Ellis Flint remarked, glancing sideways to Kempston Hardwick as if seeking agreement or approval.

'Not if ticket sales are anything to go by. Sold eighty so far. Sure, a few'll turn up and want tickets on the door, but there's no way it's even going to pay for his appearance fee, never mind the bleedin' brandy he's knocking back in there.'

'Maybe you could make a little extra cash on the side, eh?' Again, Ellis Flint looked at Kempston Hardwick for some sort of reassurance.

'How do you mean?'

'Well, there's a few people who'd still love to meet him, me for one. How about I add a tenner to your coffers and me and my new mate Kempston here can go backstage and meet him for a few minutes?'

Hardwick's eyebrow raised at Flint's casual bonding, but he said nothing.

'Call it twenty and you can have all bloody night with him, for all I care,' the landlord replied.

The deal done, Ellis Flint enthusiastically grabbed Hardwick by the arm and led him round towards the back room of the pub, via the kitchen door.

'You seem to know the place well,' Hardwick remarked, smoothing the sleeve of his winter coat.

'Oh, yes. Come here quite a lot. Helps me to unwind. Helped Doug out in the kitchen a few times, actually.'

Hardwick noted the landlord's name for future reference.

As they reached the solid beech door with the tarnished brass "PRIVATE" plate on it, Hardwick cleared his throat as Ellis Flint knocked, waited barely a nanosecond for a reply which was not forthcoming quickly enough, then entered the room.

The man whom Hardwick assumed to be Charlie Sparks was tapping a cigarette out into an ashtray, a magazine containing images of scantily-clad women sprawled on the desk in front of him.

'Ah, good timing. Another brandy, will you?' Charlie Sparks said.

'Oh, I'm afraid we're not members of staff,' Ellis explained.

'Well, bugger off out of my dressing room, then.'

'Actually, we're quite big fans of yours. We just wondered if we might be able to say hello.'

Charlie Sparks's demeanour changed visibly, as did Hardwick's, although for entirely different reasons.

'Ah, I see. Well, of course. Always a pleasure to meet my fans. Do you come to many of the live shows?' Charlie Sparks spoke intermittently between licking envelopes and stuffing them with signed photographs of himself.

Ellis Flint shuffled awkwardly as he tried to think of a suitable yet inoffensive response. As much as he admired the man's fame, he wasn't one to pay good money to follow him around the country. Hardwick sensed Flint's discomfort and threw a curve-ball at Charlie Sparks, who wasn't really paying much attention anyway.

'You must have quite a lot of fans. Do you get a lot of requests for photographs?'

'Well, not many, no. I'm somewhat less in the public eye than I used to be, y'know what I mean?'

Hardwick murmured. He was never sure how to respond to this idiomatic turn, if it required a response at all.

'My agent tends to sort out that sort of thing. Speaking of which, he should be here by now, the lazy bugger.'

Hardwick empathised with Charlie Sparks's disapproval of poor timekeeping, but this was overshadowed by his contempt for casual swearing. He tried to restrain the reflexive curling of his upper lip.

Ellis Flint nodded his understanding, not quite sure of what could be said in response.

'Anyway, time waits for no man. Going to have to love you and leave you, lads. The show must go on.' Charlie Sparks rose and ran a hand through his Grecian-2000-laden hair before he turned on the ball of his foot, his shoes scuffing on the concrete floor as he headed for the door. 'Thanks for coming to see me, lads. Really appreciate it.'

Hardwick could tell that Charlie Sparks meant every word. For a man who had once enjoyed such fame and fortune and since fallen from grace, it was rather humbling that a simple visit from two strangers could brighten his evening. Not wanting to develop too much admiration for the man, Hardwick held the door open and followed Charlie Sparks and Ellis Flint back towards the main bar.

2

Hardwick ordered another large Campari and orange, straining to make his mellow voice heard above the noise of his fellow drinkers and the Alice Cooper song which had just come on the jukebox. Barely thirty seconds in, the music was cut as Doug, the landlord, began tapping the microphone and attempted to count beyond two. A shaven-headed youth at the back of the pub expressed his disapproval of having wasted 'two soddin' quid' on the jukebox barely seconds earlier. Doug responded with the sentiment that the eight o'clock start had been pretty darned-well advertised, if he might say so himself.

Still unable to get beyond the number two, Doug resorted to booming the word 'testing' into the microphone over and over at a volume and pitch much lower, and a distance much closer, than anyone was likely to speak into the microphone all night. The equipment supposedly adjusted, Doug addressed the crowd with a 'GOOD E—' before stopping to adjust the equipment again following the loud boom and ear-piercing screech which emanated from every speaker in the building.

The assembled crowd still rubbing their ears and mopping up their drinks, Doug tried the microphone a second time.

'Good evening, ladies and gentlemen.' Small screech. 'Welcome to the Freemason's Arms.' Another small screech made it sound as though he said 'Freemason's Arse'. 'We have for you tonight a man who is known the world over. A man who is a household name throughout the country thanks to game shows such as Mind That Bell and Charlie's Going Ape. Many of you will be aware that he's also a legend on the stand-up circuit, so we're very pleased to have him here tonight. Ladies and gentlemen, Mr Charlie Sparks!'

The crowd reacted with a mixture of spattered applause and the odd sarcastic whistle as Charlie Sparks took to the stage. It wasn't long before Kempston Hardwick's teeth started to itch at the blue "humour".

'Evening all. My wife's just started doing some exercise to lose some weight. She went out jogging the other day and stopped all of a sudden, thinking she'd had a heart attack as she had a sharp shooting pain under her left breast. Turns out she'd sprained her knee.' The rotund jovial barflies nodded their ascent vigorously through hearty belly laughs. 'I had the best dump of my life earlier today,' the comedian went on. 'It managed to touch the water before breaking off. I think you'll agree that's pretty damned impressive from the middle diving board.'

Hardwick was mildly disheartened at the sight of Ellis Flint chuckling to himself at the two opening jokes, but then he wasn't all that surprised.

'Not your sort of humour, Kempston?' Ellis Flint remarked, having caught Hardwick's eye.

'I'm not really one for comedy,' came the response. 'Not of this type, anyway.'

'More of a sit-com man, are you?'

'Aristophanes and Menander, mainly.'

'Not heard of them. BBC Three, are they?'

'More 3 BC, actually.'

'Not sure I've heard of that one. Get all sorts on digital these days.'

Hardwick murmured a non-committal noise and ordered another drink. As his eyes flitted from Ellis Flint towards the bar, they passed the focal point of Charlie Sparks, whereupon Hardwick noticed that he seemed to be perspiring profusely, his head and arms beginning to jerk.

'I used to go out with a Welsh girl who had thirty-six double-Ds,' the comedian began to slur. 'All got such stupidly long names, the Welsh, haven't they?' Charlie Sparks stood and held a smile as the audience lapped up his latest quip. Hardwick had barely noticed that the smile had been more than a little too drawn out when Charlie Sparks's feet started to buckle under him, the bulbous man's not-inconsiderable weight seeming to cause him some stability problems. A few moments of confusion reigned for the audience as he descended from the stage with an excruciated look on his face and headed towards his dressing room. Charlie Sparks was a man known for the occasional stage antics, but Hardwick was less than convinced.

'Something's not right. Something's terribly wrong,' he remarked to no-one in particular before following the comedian. His first thoughts turning towards preserving the scene, Hardwick cautioned the concerned bystanders to keep back.

'Are you a doctor, mate?' came the voice of a front-row audience member. 'It's all right, I think he's a doctor.'

Ellis Flint joined Hardwick backstage, whereupon he found Hardwick knelt at the side of Charlie Sparks, who lay contorted on the concrete floor.

'Is he breathing?' Ellis asked.

'No. He's dead.' Hardwick's eyes didn't leave Charlie Sparks's sweaty, lifeless body.

'Heart attack?'

'It somehow seems unlikely,' Hardwick remarked, his suspicions aroused. 'Oh no, this was quite clever. Quite clever indeed. Faster acting than usual. I dare say the dose must have been substantial.'

'Dose of what, Kempston? What's going on?'

'Look, Ellis! Can't you see? The man's face! Risus sardonicus, the maniacal grin of a man gripped by tetanus poisoning!'

'Tetanus? Bloody hell. What happened, did he cut himself?'

'Oh, I very much doubt it. Judging by the speed of the reaction, this was no small dose. Certainly nothing which could have been administered by accident. Ellis, we're looking at a crime scene.'

'Crime scene? Right,' Ellis Flint said, as he rose to his feet and addressed the crowd which had now assembled outside the dressing room. 'I'm afraid we'll need everyone out of the building, ladies and gentlemen,' he bellowed to the thronging crowds.

'No!' came the bark from Hardwick. 'No-one is to leave the building!'

'Are you a police officer, mate?' came the familiar

voice from the audience. 'It's all right, I think he's a police officer.'

Hardwick slanted his head towards Ellis Flint. 'Lock the doors. Let no-one escape.'

Ellis Flint, his excitement roused, nodded and left the room.

3

'What happened, officer?' Hardwick looked up at the pub landlord, not saying a word. 'Doug Lilley, I'm the landlord here.'

'We met earlier tonight.'

'What's your name?'

'Hardwick.'

'PC Hardwick? DS Hardwick?'

'Kempston Hardwick.'

'Ooh, like one of those surgeons who's gone beyond Dr and reverts back to Mr, then.'

'Something like that, yes.'

'So what the hell happened?'

'Charlie Sparks is dead, Mr Lilley.'

'I can bloody well see that, officer. I mean how the hell did he die?'

'If I knew that, I wouldn't be knelt here now. I'll need to speak to everyone here. Gather everyone together and get their names, please.'

'What, all of them? We close in two hours.'

'You're closed now, Mr Lilley. And we'll remain here for as long as it takes. Ellis, I'll need you to help me with the interview process,' he said, as Doug Lilley stepped out of the room and began to usher the crowds to the far end of the Freemason's Arms.

'You didn't mention you were a police officer, you dirty old dog, you,' Flint said.

'No. There's a reason for that.'

'Undercover work, is it?'

'Not a million miles from the truth. Unlike this man's death, it seems. I think it's about time we started interviewing people. No time like the present.'

'What about the body?'

'I've seen what I need to see. You can call the police now.'

'The police? I thought you said you were the police.'

'I can assure you I didn't, dear boy. First of all, I'll need to speak with Mr Lilley, the landlord.'

'Are you sure it's a good idea to be interviewing people if you're not a police officer?'

'I don't think you'll find it's against the law. With a

bit of luck, we'll have this matter sewn up before the brakes are warm on the Panda car.'

Hardwick stood and straightened his coat before heading into the main bar, beckoning to Doug Lilley with a come-hither finger. Leading the landlord into the kitchen to behind the bar of the Freemason's Arms, Hardwick folded his arms and leant against the brushed metal work surface.

'How long had you known Charlie Sparks, Mr Lilley?'

'Known him? About an hour, since he first turned up here before the gig. If you mean how long had I known of him, then like most people in this pub I'd reckon a good twenty-five years or so. He was a massive star in his day.'

'So I'm led to believe. What was the impetus behind Charlie Sparks playing here tonight?'

'His manager, guy by the name of Don Preston, lives locally. Often gets some comedians and singers and what-not in here.'

'What sort of comedians and singers?' Hardwick asked.

'All sorts, really. None as big a name as Charlie Sparks, though. Right coup, that one. He lives pretty locally himself, see. Over in Fettlesham, apparently.' Hardwick noted the location of the village in his mind's eye. 'There's not really much more I can tell you, officer. I'm afraid you'll need to speak to his manager if you want to find out more about him.' Doug Lilley handed Hardwick a business card with Don Preston's details emblazoned on it.

'Right. Well, thank you for your time, Mr Lilley. I'm sure the police will be along shortly and will probably want to speak to you as well.'

'Police? Then who are you?'

4

'Ellis, I'll need you to come with me. We need to go and speak to Charlie Sparks's manager, a Don Preston. Lives over at Little Markham.'

'Right-o. What about speaking to all these people?'

'I'm not sure any of them will be much use. The police will be along soon to speak to them.'

Ellis Flint stopped dead in his tracks. 'Just who are you, exactly, Kempston? Are you a police officer?'

'Certainly not.'

'So what are you? Some kind of investigator?'

'Just a civilian with a nose for suspicion and a hunger for the truth, Ellis. Now, we'd better hail a cab.'

* * *

'Come on then,' Ellis Flint asked once they were both settled inside the taxi. 'Tell me about you.'

'There's absolutely nothing to tell.'

'Well that's clearly not true. You were in the Freemason's Arms tonight for a reason, and you seem to have some sort of nose for death.'

'I've had worse things said about me,' Hardwick replied nonchalantly.

'Well, don't you want to know about me?' Ellis asked.

'Not especially. Besides, I already know most of the pertinent information.'

'Such as?'

'You're married — wedding ring. You're over the age of forty — the hair on your shins is thinning.' As Hardwick spoke, Ellis Flint's eyes darted to his trousers, which he coyly pulled back over his cotton socks. 'You're currently out of work — you jumped at the chance to carry out a murder investigation with a complete stranger and you were already half-cut by six o'clock on a Friday afternoon. Besides, I noticed you had a Saver-Market receipt in a rather expensive Italian leather wallet. Someone who can afford such luxury is only likely to shop at SaverMarket if he's currently out of work. Oh, and you had an upper-middle-class upbringing and you served some time in the Army.'

Hardwick was quite certain that the taxi driver had made the short journey to Little Markham far longer than it needed to be. Not ever having driven a car himself, he couldn't be totally sure, but he knew when he was being taken for a ride, as it were.

'How on earth did you know about my upbringing and Army background?' Ellis Flint asked.

'You use some peculiar turns of phrase, for a start. I don't imagine you ever felt comfortable with your upbringing, and you certainly try to hide it but that makes it so much more discernible.'

'And the Army thing?'

'Well, you were a bit of a fan of Charlie Sparks. You said so yourself, yet you didn't seem at all fazed by his sudden death. Plus, you seem like a man fulfilled, Ellis,' Hardwick said, raising a satisfied smile from Ellis Flint. 'Besides which, you seem to show remarkable deference to any tall stranger in a brown suit.'

Little Markham was the archetypal chocolate-box village, with large stone walls seemingly made from marshmallows, Hansel and Gretel cottages lining the streets with their dew-dampened thatched roofs glistening in the moonlight. The taxi turned into Wood

View and Hardwick and Flint alighted outside number three. The house looked remarkably modern in comparison to the surrounding cottages on the high street, but Hardwick supposed it must still be a good couple of hundred years old. The lead-lined windows gave an air of security and substance that no modern building could ever replicate.

Don Preston opened the door barely a few moments after the doorbell had chimed, to find the two men stood beneath the wisteria that framed the studded wooden door.

'Good evening. Don Preston?'

'Yes, can I help you, gentlemen?'

'My name is D.I. Kempston Hardwick and this is Ellis Flint. We need to speak to you about Charlie Sparks. I believe you represent him.'

'Oh right, yes. Come on in.'

Hardwick and Flint were led into Don Preston's living room. A collection of horse brasses decorated the black-beamed hearth that surrounded the fireplace, and a widescreen television was the only reminder of the current era.

'Can I get you a cup of tea, chaps? Actually, it's a bit late, isn't it? Something a little stronger, perhaps?'

'We'll be fine, thank you, Mr Preston,' Hardwick answered. Ellis Flint raised his eyebrow momentarily at the thought of being spoken for with regards to a free drink.

'So, what's the silly old bugger done now? Got himself in some sort of fight again? I mean, I'm presuming you're both police officers. Don't often get door-to-door calls around here at this time of night. Even Betterware have given up!' Don Preston chuckled.

Hardwick ignored the assumption. 'I presume you were aware that Charlie Sparks had been performing at the Freemason's Arms earlier tonight?'

'Yes, absolutely. I arranged it for him, as I do with all of his gigs.'

'I'm afraid there's been a bit of a mishap,' Hardwick understated. 'Charlie Sparks collapsed and died whilst on stage tonight, Mr Preston.'

Don Preston's previous smile slowly became more subdued as the reality of what had been said seemed to set in. 'Died? Is this some sort of joke?'

About as tasteful as most of his, Hardwick thought to himself. 'I'm afraid not. What's more, it seems as though he died in suspicious circumstances.'

'Suspicious?'

'Yes. Unfortunately, we believe he may have been murdered.'

'Oh, Jesus Christ. Sorry, but this... this is just... oh my, I'm not quite sure what to say.'

'There's probably not a whole lot more to say at this stage, Mr Preston. However, we'll need to speak to anyone who was close to Charlie Sparks. Just as a matter of course, you understand.'

'Well yes, of course.'

'You'll need some time to come to terms with what's happened,' Ellis Flint spoke up, until now having remained uncharacteristically silent but beginning to get into his new role as a sleuth. 'However, we'll need details of his family and close acquaintances in order to begin investigating what happened.'

'I understand. It's just so shocking. I've known him since university. I really don't know what to say. I can only suggest that you should probably speak to his wife first of all. She deserves to be informed, if you haven't already.'

'We were hoping that you would be able to put us in touch, Mr Preston,' Hardwick stated.

'Naturally. Marianne, her name is. They... she... lives at Manor Farm in Fettlesham.'

'Thank you, Mr Preston. We'll be in touch in due course.'

'Yes, of course. Please do call if I can be of any assistance. If I think of anything else that may help, I'll call the station and ask to speak with you.'

'Probably not a good idea, Mr Preston. You can reach

me on this number,' Hardwick said, passing Don Preston his remarkably simple calling card:

KEMPSTON HARDWICK
01632 960555

When they were back outside, Ellis took Hardwick by the arm and glared at him with a look of anger.

'Kempston! You can't just go around impersonating a police officer! It's illegal! You'll have us banged up!'

'Yes, I know. That's why I didn't impersonate a police officer, Ellis.'

'What? "I'm D.I. Kempston Hardwick"? Sounded pretty conclusive to me.'

'I didn't lie, Ellis. My birth name is Dagwood Isambard Kempston Hardwick. I simply chose to include the first two initials of my name when introducing myself. If those were your three forenames, Ellis, which one would you use?'

5

Fettlesham seemed a million miles away from Little Markham, although geographically fewer than four miles separated them. Gone were the period cottages, but for a few; the majority destroyed by an overturned petrol-tanker in the 1970s, as was Hardwick's understanding. Manor Farm stood on the edge of the village, a tragically modern, if large, house, set deliriously distant from any nearby farm of the traditional naming convention. Having been deposited outside Manor Farm by the same taxi driver who had driven them to Little Markham, Hardwick and Flint made their way up the noisy gravel driveway to the front door. The large bay windows allowed a reasonable view of the living room, the tell-tale flicker and glow of a television set letting them know that Charlie Sparks's wife was likely still awake.

Hardwick raised not a smile at the inappropriate jovial bounce of the Benny Hill theme tune which played as he pressed the plastic doorbell. The woman who answered the door was an unexpectedly bouncy-looking lady, more accustomed to a Les Dawson character than anything ever dreamt up by Benny Hill.

'Good evening, madam. Mrs Sparks, I presume?'

'After a fashion, yes. Can I help you two at all?'

'Yes, it's your husband we'd like to speak with you about. May we come in?'

'Well, that depends. Are you police officers?'

Hardwick thought for a moment. 'After a fashion.'

She seemed to deem this a suitable response, opening the door further to allow Hardwick and Flint to enter the house. She elaborated on entering the living room, having deigned to switch off the flickering television screen. 'Charlie Sparks is just a stage name, you see. His real name is Dave Spencer and I'm Marianne.'

'I see. Any reason behind the stage name?'

'Well, Dave Spencer doesn't exactly set the world alight in the same way as Sparks, does it?'

Hardwick said nothing, assuming that Marianne Spencer's own unintentional pun was lost on her.

'So, what's this all about, anyway?' Marianne asked. 'You mentioned something to do with Dave.'

'Yes. I'm sorry to have to tell you that Ch... Dave, collapsed on stage earlier this evening. I'm sorry, Mrs Spencer, but he passed away.'

'Oh my... I... oh dear... What happened?' Marianne Spencer seemed shocked and surprised, yet not remarkably upset.

'We're not quite sure yet. It's possible that something... might not have agreed with him.'

Hardwick looked at Flint. Flint looked at Hardwick. The thought was mutually agreed, but unspoken between the two men.

'Wh... who have you told?'

'Well, naturally we would have come to speak to you first, but we only found out your whereabouts after speaking with Don Preston, his manager,' Hardwick replied.

'Oh, poor Don!'

'I presume he has some family to console him?' Ellis Flint offered.

'I... well, yes. He has a step-son.'

'I realise you may need some more time to come to terms with what's happened, but when you're ready we'd like to speak to you a little more about your husband.'

'Well, yes. It has come as a terrible shock. I really don't know what to say.'

'Did your husband have any enemies, Mrs Spencer?'

Charlie Sparks's wife let out a half-cry, half-laugh at this, and began shaking her head. 'Where should I begin? He was hardly a popular man in many circles, officer.'

'Actually, we're...' Hardwick placed a hand on Ellis Flint's arm, as if to stop him mid-sentence.

'But what does that have to do with his death?' Marianne Spencer asked.

'We have reason to believe that your husband may have been murdered, Mrs Spencer.'

Marianne Spencer looked at the carpet and simply nodded, slowly. Another mutual glance was shared between the two men. 'I'd like to tell you I'm shocked and surprised. The truth of the matter is, Dave had upset a great many people throughout his life. He was the archetypal failed has-been entertainer. If you want a list of people you should speak to, I'm afraid you'll need a rather large sheet of paper.' The tears welled up in Marianne Spencer's eyes as she said this, yet not one drop dared to make the first leap of faith towards her not-inconsiderable cheeks.

'Do you have any children, Mrs Spencer?' Ellis Flint attempted to cut through the deepening and darkening atmosphere. Marianne Spencer simply laughed at this apparent affront.

'Not bloody likely. He had what some might call *Ascension* Deficit Disorder.'

Ellis Flint cocked his head to the side.

'Have you ever tried to turn the kitchen tap on when your pipes are frozen, officer? Well that's what my husband's d—'

'Yes! Well, that's a terrible shame, Mrs Spencer. How very unfortunate,' Hardwick jumped in with a slight raise in pitch to his voice. 'And may I ask how you both met?'

'Noah's bloody ark, I think. Feels that long, anyway.' Hardwick told himself off for trying to imagine which two animals the Spencers would have represented. 'I used to be a dancer on his Saturday night show back in the seventies. Fact is, he used to be a bit of a playboy in his day. I took great delight in being the one who managed to rein him in and turn him into a family man. There's bloody irony for you.'

'Were you married long?'

'Too bloody long. Thirty years last August. It's not been without its ups and downs, though, I can assure you.' Hardly the revelation of the century, Hardwick thought. 'Dave Spencer was a failure as a husband, a failure as a father, and a failure as a businessman.' Marianne Spencer seemed to speak with more than a slight air of contempt for her recently deceased husband.

'What business interests did he have, exactly?'

'Most recently he was a partner in a company called Wellington Pharmaceuticals with an old school friend of his, Patrick Allen. Another way for him to waste all of the money he'd earned in his hey-day.'

'Would you say your husband was careless with money?'

'Oh, God, yes. Look at the cars he's got out there. And the fact that for years he's been pumping money into that bloody company. We've got nothing left now. Nothing but a load of debt, anyway.'

'And where were you earlier this evening, Mrs Spencer?'

'I've been sat here all night. I'm sorry, gentlemen, but my husband was a liar, a cheat and a worm. Anyone will tell you that. The one thing I can tell you, though, is that I had nothing to do with his death.'

Having been shown out of the house by an amicable Marianne Spencer, Hardwick and Flint made their way up towards Fettlesham High Street.

'Do you think she had anything to do with it, Kempston?'

'I don't know. All I do know is that there's an awful lot that we still have to find out. I have a funny feeling that this is going to open up quite a can of worms for poor Charlie Sparks. It doesn't seem that he led the most pious of lives.'

'Does anyone?' Ellis Flint asked.

Hardwick said nothing, and slowed his pace momentarily as he extracted a Montecristo No. 2 and lit it delicately with a match.

'What's the next move, then?' Ellis Flint asked.

Hardwick looked at his watch. 'It's five to eleven, so I think we've time for a night-cap at the Fox & Bugle on the high street. In the morning, however, I think we'd better pay a visit to Charlie Sparks's business partner, Patrick Allen.'

6

The solitary shaft of moonlight that peered between the long curtains played on Hardwick's glass as he swirled the liquid within it. He stared into nothingness, the sheer silence deafening his every thought, a thousand-and-one of which whirled around his head like the drink in his glass.

The occasional rumbling of the wind through the trees kept Hardwick just this side of reality, although the super-powered telescope of his mind's eye was still well-focused on other things. He had always tried not to let it shape him, but he felt his back teeth beginning to grind as his breathing got heavier.

It had given him his drive and determination. For that, he could be thankful. The indefatigable motivation to seek justice and retribution wherever it could be sought. The overriding compulsion that bad people could, and should, not get away with bad things.

He knew not if the passing time was that of seconds, minutes or hours. Even the mostly-unnoticed ticking of the grandfather clock gave no indication of time passed.

The thoughts came back to him every now and again. The train station. The hard, brown suitcase, its lacquer peeling back to reveal fraying board. The liquorice bonbons. The shrill, piercing screech of the steam whistle. *All aboard. Mind the gap, please.* The thought that something terrible was happening; had happened. Those same, breathtakingly painful thoughts which rearer their ugly heads at times like these. Terror and injustice. Bad people. Bad thoughts.

A solitary tear ran from his eye.

7

Shortly after morning broke, Hardwick and Flint found themselves heading back in the direction of Fettlesham, again having travelled by way of taxi at Hardwick's unexplained request.

'You know, Kempston, I was thinking last night.'

Hardwick made a non-committal murmur.

'The thing is, I realised that I don't actually know anything about you. I mean, it feels like I've known you for ages but at the same time I don't even know who you are.'

'Who is anybody?' Hardwick replied, not taking his eyes from that day's copy of *The Times*.

'Well, that's a good point. Perhaps a tad too philo-sophical for a Saturday morning, but still. What do you actually do? I mean, do you do this detective stuff regularly?'

'People don't tend to get murdered regularly,' Hardwick said, forcing a raised eyebrow from Ellis Flint.

'No, but I mean have you ever done this before?'

'By definition, no. No two murders are ever the same. That's the beauty of life, Ellis. There's even beauty in murder, if you look closely enough.' Hardwick's eyes didn't leave the newspaper, instead staring blankly at the same three words for a few moments before he lowered the paper and spoke again to Flint. 'You're quite keen, aren't you?'

'Sorry?'

'I mean, you had no need to get involved with this investigation, did you? You didn't know Charlie Sparks personally and you'd never met me until last night.'

'Well, it's exciting stuff, isn't it? Truth is, it's always sort of appealed to me, this line of work. I used to love detective books when I was a kid. I remember one, it was clearly aimed at children: the cases involved stolen balloons and housekeepers pretending to be ghosts. All innocent stuff in the grand scheme of things, but that's what gave me my love of mystery stories.'

'I see. And do you often manage to spot the villain before the end?' Hardwick asked.

'Never, if I'm honest. I hope that doesn't reflect badly.'

'Not at all. Quite the opposite, in fact. The truth is, murders just don't happen the way they're written in books. The vast majority of murder cases are very simple and straightforward. No red herrings, no cases of mistaken identity, no switching of clocks or mirrors. Most of the time, instinct prevails.'

'Is it not usually the spouse of the victim who committed the murder?' Ellis asked.

'Most of the time, yes,' Hardwick replied. 'But that would make life very boring indeed.'

Patrick Allen's house sat back from the road on White's Lane, a red-brick wall holding the iron gate shut as the mock-Tudor house poked out from the immaculate lawn behind. It was Ellis Flint who pressed the intercom button on the gate's control panel.

'Hello?'

'Good morning. My name's Kempston Hardwick and this is Ellis Flint. We're here to speak to Mr Allen about Dave Spencer, also known as Charlie Sparks.'

No further words were said, but moments later the gates began to roll apart as the house exposed itself to the two men like a prize on a game-show. Passing the gleaming Range Rover Sport parked on the tarmacked driveway, Hardwick and Flint had barely travelled two thirds of the way down the front path before the door opened and a tall man who seemed to be greying before his time stepped out onto the doormat.

'Hi, I'm Patrick Allen. Terrible news about Dave.'

'You've heard?'

'Yes, his wife called me last night. Couldn't quite believe it myself. I only saw him yesterday afternoon before he went off for his gig. I'm afraid I'm not really sure what to say.'

'Well, if you don't mind, Mr Allen, we'd like to come in and ask you a few questions.'

'Oh yes, of course. Do come in.'

The interior of Patrick Allen's house was tastefully decorated, if a little too clinically clean. The contrast between the traditional cottages of Little Markham and the modern mansions of Fettlesham was yet again apparent to Kempston Hardwick as he glanced around the kitchen at the immaculate work surfaces and over-abundance of white. Hardwick abhorred white, seeing it as a soulless, unnecessary colour.

'We understand that you were a business partner of Dave Spencer's, Mr Allen.'

'You could say that, yes. We run — ran — a company called Wellington Pharmaceuticals. Known Dave since we were both at school together. That's why it's come as a bit of a shock, if I'm honest.'

'And how has the company been performing?'

'About as well as any company is these days, I suppose. It's had its ups and downs, but it's provided an income for the last good few years, so I can't really complain.'

'Were there any other shareholders?'

'No, just the two of us. Dave was more of a silent partner, just tended to provide the funding when it was needed and helped the business to get off the ground and expand. I mean, he had his own office and did the occasional few days, but I take care of the day-to-day running of the company.'

'And how many staff do you have working for you, Mr Allen?'

'Twenty at the moment. Mostly sales and office staff, as well as an IT and accounts guy who works from the basement. We don't tend to do much in the way of research. Just tends to be direct sales to the medical and research industries.'

Hardwick mulled this over for a few moments, trying to gauge the direction in which the conversation should go. On the face of it, it seemed that Patrick Allen had done very well for himself through his involvement with Wellington Pharmaceuticals. He had an expensive car sat on his driveway and the home was decorated lavishly with contemporary ornaments — perhaps a little too modern for Hardwick's tastes, but undeniably costly.

'Do you live here alone, Mr Allen?'

'Goodness, no. My wife, Anne-Marie, is at work.'

'No children?'

'Not at home, no. We have two, but they both have their own families now.'

'Rather a large house for the two of you, isn't it?'

'Indeed, but we both love it to pieces. Anne-Marie, especially. I don't think either of us could imagine living anywhere else.'

Somewhere with a little less white gloss paint, Hardwick thought to himself.

Once the meeting had concluded and the pair had left Patrick Allen's sumptuous property, Hardwick was somewhat taken aback by the force with which Ellis Flint had grabbed him by the pleats of his coat and thrust him at a nearby bush. Still holding onto Hardwick's coat, Ellis Flint's face had an air of revelation.

'Don't you see? My God, it's all coming together already, Kempston! Patrick Allen said he and Charlie Sparks were the sole owners of Wellington Pharmaceuticals. That means, if one of the pair were to die, the other would gain sole control of the company!'

'That's hardly a motive for murder, though,' Hardwick protested, squirming free of his grip and dusting off his coat.

'Absolutely not. There's almost certainly something else. But I'd be willing to bet that the fortunes of Wellington Pharmaceuticals aren't quite as they seem.'

8

Ellis Flint sat in his study and tapped at his laptop's black-on-white keys furiously. His password entered, he selected his favoured internet browser and entered "poisons" into the search engine. He was met with a selection of encyclopaedia entries, medical journals and NHS links, most of which seemed far too daunting for the little information he needed, which was what poison could possibly have killed Charlie Sparks.

That any poison in the world was readily available to Patrick Allen by means of his company being one of the country's major stockists of chemicals was undeniable, but how on earth could it be proved? Naturally, the sheer range and number of chemicals and substances available on the premises of Wellington Pharmaceuticals should mean that any possible combination of poisons, explosives, potions and medicines could be easily created by someone with prior knowledge.

The subject matter was simply too vast to take in all at once. It was like looking for a needle in a haystack. What on Earth could be given internally which would cause tetanus poisoning? He decided he needed some expert advice. Without taking a moment to think, he dialled the number of the local police station and asked to speak to someone about methods of poisoning.

'Can I ask what this is in relation to, sir?' the understandably cautious desk sergeant asked.

'It's to do with a murder case you're currently investigating.'

'May I ask which one?'

'Charlie Sparks, otherwise known as Dave Spencer.'

'One moment please.'

After twenty or thirty seconds of being told that his call was important to them, Flint found himself talking to a deep-voiced man who introduced himself as Detective Inspector Rob Warner.

'You say you have some information regarding a murder case, sir?'

'Well, more questions, actually. It's about the Dave Spencer case.'

'I see. I think it's probably best if we discuss this at your place.'

Ellis Flint beamed with excitement at the prospect of moving one step ahead of Hardwick and diligently provided DI Warner with his address. Following the conclusion of the call, he called Hardwick to tell him the good news.

'You bloody fool!' Hardwick spluttered. 'What on earth did you do that for?'

'What's the matter, Kempston? We're almost there! With the police's help, or them with our help, we can help find Charlie Sparks's murderer!'

'Fool!' Hardwick informed Flint that he would be at his place as quickly as possible and slammed down the telephone.

* * *

Arriving barely a minute before the police officers, Hardwick had little opportunity to explain his rage to Flint, leaving him with an uncomfortably small amount of space between Hardwick and the wall of the hallway.

'What on earth possessed you to do such a thing?' Hardwick asked.

'Are you mad, man? We can help the police investigate Charlie Sparks's murder!'

'As far as the police are concerned, there is no murder to investigate, you fool! All they have managed to garner is that Charlie Sparks died on stage and that no cause of death has yet been decided. If you go wading in with accusations of murder, all hell could break loose!'

'But you told me you thought he'd been murdered!'

'And I do! I know he was murdered! But as things stand, we're the only two souls who do, so where do you think that puts us in terms of suspects numbers one and two?'

'Ah, I see. Well that's put us in a bit of a pickle.'

'You fool, Flint. You absolute—'

Only the ringing of the doorbell could cut the atmosphere. As Ellis Flint eased himself from between Hardwick and the wall and opened the front door, he could hear Hardwick's footsteps retreating towards the living room, rhythmically accompanied by his whispered curses.

The man who introduced himself as Detective Inspector Rob Warner was a tall, portly man with a comical comb-over. He introduced his fellow officer as Detective Constable Sam Kerrigan. DC Kerrigan was a young officer, barely out of school, it seemed, but he carried with him an air of confidence and bravado which Hardwick immediately recognised as the folly of youth.

'Mr Flint, we believe you wanted to speak to us about a potential murder case?'

'Well, sort of,' Ellis Flint started, glancing at Hardwick, who stood coyly in the doorway to the living room. 'It's actually more of a question I had. A few questions, actually.'

'Right. Are they the sort of questions you feel comfortable asking in front of your... friend?' DI Warner looked at Hardwick and spoke the last word with an air of implication.

'Oh, sorry. Yes, this is Kempston Hardwick. A good friend of mine.' Ellis Flint led the two officers towards the living room.

'Good friend, right. Very nice to meet you, Kempston.' DI Warner moved to extend his hand but decided against it.

'Hardwick,' came the sole response.

'Right. Mr Hardwick. Well, shall we go into the living room?' DI Warner half-attempted to squeeze past Hardwick at the living-room door whilst gesturing for him to enter first, raising his eyebrows in unison with DC Kerrigan as he followed Hardwick into the room.

'Tell us, Mr Flint, what questions did you have?'

'Well, it's about poisons, really.'

'Poisons?'

'Yes, poisons. I was wondering if there was a particular poison that might cause a person to get very ill and die quite suddenly.'

DI Warner laughed before answering. 'Only a few

hundred thousand. Why do you want to know, exactly? This could easily be considered to be a waste of police time.'

Hardwick thought he would be better off answering the question. 'Well, it's quite simple. It's for a... Uh...'

'School project,' Flint interjected, with very little in the way of prior thought.

'A school project?' DI Warner asked.

'Well, college course,' Flint responded, noticing that Hardwick now had his head buried deep in his hands. 'I'm doing a college course and wanted to get some extra background information.'

'I see. What college course is it?'

'Poisons. Well, chemistry. Chemicals and poisons. Actually, you know, it doesn't matter. I can probably find the information on the internet.'

'Mr Flint, this is a very serious matter. Our police department is extremely understaffed at the present time and we can't simply start sending out officers every time someone wants to ask us some inane questions. We really are very busy.'

'No, yes, I understand. I'm very sorry. Next time I'll carry out my own research.'

'Very well. Now, on to the matter of Charlie Sparks.' Hardwick and Flint glanced at each other, both hoping that the conversation wouldn't move on to this subject.

'You mentioned on the phone that you wanted to speak to us about some information.'

'Well, no. That was a mistake. It was just about the poisons, that's all.'

'Mr Flint, you told our desk sergeant that you were calling about the murder of Charlie Sparks.'

'I see. Yes, slip of the tongue, I'm afraid. Just the poisons.'

'Mr Flint, we're not investigating any murder in relation to the death of Charlie Sparks,' DI Warner said, standing and moving towards the door. 'The reasons for his death are unknown, but he was an overweight man. A smoker and a drinker. Needless to say, we're not currently treating his death as suspicious. Of course, should that change, you'll be the first to know,' he added with a thinly-veiled threat.

As DI Warner walked back down the steps from Ellis Flint's house, the up-until-now quiet DC Sam Kerrigan leant in and half-whispered to Flint: 'I'd keep your nose out if I were you. Police business don't concern you.'

'Doesn't,' Hardwick corrected, not taking his eyes from the ceiling.

'I beg your pardon?'

'Police work *doesn't* concern us. Is a basic grasp of

the English language not a requirement in the police force nowadays?'

DC Kerrigan stared at Hardwick for a few moments before raising a cocky smile and, thrusting his hands into his pockets, began to follow DI Warner down the steps, turning only to add: 'We'll be seeing you again, gents.'

The door closed, Flint postulated, 'So what do we do now?'

'Nothing,' Hardwick responded. 'That is to say, nothing different. We just need to make sure we keep away from the noses of Detective Inspector Warner and Detective Constable Kerrigan while we continue our own investigations.'

'Good idea. The fact that the police aren't even yet treating Charlie Sparks's death as suspicious says to me that we've something of a head-start,' Flint added.

'It's not a competition,' Hardwick responded. 'It's the pure and simple fact that somewhere out there, a killer is on the loose. And we're the only two people in the world who are looking for him.'

'Or her,' Flint remarked.

'Indeed. Or her,' Hardwick murmured pensively.

9

The late-afternoon sky had turned a mellow purple and the almost-faded light cast silhouettes all the way to the horizon. Hardwick's house was silent but for the rhythmic ticking of the grandfather clock in the hallway.

He sat looking at a notebook which he could barely see in the low light, yet he knew exactly what the words said. Exhaling and removing his reading glasses, Hardwick reached for the bakelite telephone and dialled the number.

'Mr Allen, it's Kempston Hardwick here. We spoke at your house regarding the death of Charlie Sparks.'

'Ah yes, good to hear from you. Have you caught the killer yet?'

'No, but we do need to ask you for some more information if we may. Is it convenient to meet tomorrow morning?'

'Yes, but not at home. Can we meet somewhere else?'

'Absolutely. How does the Freemason's Arms sound?' Hardwick suggested, listening for any hint of emotion in Patrick Allen's voice.

'Well, that sounds fine to me. A little out of my way, but it's neutral ground, I guess. How does 11.30 sound?'

'Perfect.'

* * *

The air hung crisp in the air as the sunshine failed to break through the morning mist. The Freemason's Arms was the only pub in the area that opened before midday, releasing its door catches at 10 o'clock every morning. Many locals remarked that this was quite odd for a small village pub, but it surprised none that Doug Lilley should have little else to do with his mornings.

Rubbing his hands warm again, Hardwick entered the pub and awaited the arrival of Patrick Allen. He ordered a large Campari and took a seat at a nearby table, at which he extracted a copy of that day's *Times* from his inside coat pocket and turned to the crossword.

When Patrick Allen did arrive, ten minutes later, Hardwick moved on immediately to the points in hand.

'Mr Allen, you told us the other day that you own Wellington Pharmaceuticals with Charlie Sparks, otherwise known as Dave Spencer,' Hardwick stated.

'Owned, yes,' Patrick Allen corrected. 'I've no idea what will happen to the company now.'

'Quite. Would you say that the chemicals stocked by your company could be quite easily used to poison a human being?'

'Well, I suppose it's always possible. Wait. Are you suggesting that I killed Dave Spencer?'

'That's a very quick conclusion to jump to, Mr Allen,' Hardwick said, his back hunching slightly as he studied the man before him. 'Tell me. Do you know of anyone who might have reason to want him dead?'

'Blimey, only a few hundred. How many names do you want?'

'Perhaps we could start with one, Mr Allen. Would I be correct in assuming that you'd stand to benefit from the victim's death by inheriting his half of the company?'

'I'm not entirely sure how the legal process would work, if I'm honest,' Patrick Allen responded. 'Besides, the company is worth bugger all nowadays.'

'Oh, I'm more than aware of that,' Hardwick said,

plunging his hand deep into his inside coat pocket yet again, this time extracting a few sheets of folded A4 paper. 'You see, I went to the lengths of obtaining your company accounts, dated just two months ago. It doesn't seem that Wellington Pharmaceuticals is doing too well at all.'

'Wait, how did you get those?'

'Wellington Pharmaceuticals is a limited company, Mr Allen. The accounts are publicly accessible.'

'Well, I know, but—'

'And do you know what else is accessible?' Hardwick asked, turning to the rearmost of his sheets of paper. Patrick Allen shook his head. 'The set of conditions by which each company is run. You see, in general company law, the remaining shares of a deceased partner would pass to the spouse of the deceased. Looking at the documents of Wellington Pharmaceuticals, it seems that a clause was added just over four months ago.' Hardwick turned the sheet of paper to face Patrick Allen and pointed to the paragraph which was circled in deep blue fountain pen ink.

4.2 *The shareholders agree that, upon the occasion of the death of any shareholder, the shares in the Company held by the deceased should be evenly distributed between the remaining shareholders.*

'That is to say, Mr Allen, that upon the death of Dave Spencer, you stood to gain the remaining fifty-percent of shares in Wellington Pharmaceuticals, becoming the sole shareholder.'

Patrick Allen simply laughed. 'Let me ask you something, Mr Hardwick. What is double bugger all?'

Hardwick had anticipated this response. 'That question assumes that the recent downturn in fortunes at Wellington Pharmaceuticals was irrevocable, Mr Allen. If you don't mind, I should like to ask you a few questions about why the company had performed so poorly recently.'

'If I knew that I wouldn't be sat here struggling to pay my bloody mortgage, would I?'

Hardwick ignored the question. 'Mr Allen, would you mind if I had a more in-depth look at your company accounts?'

'Yes, I bloody well would!' Patrick Allen shouted, rousing the attention of the one other drinker in the pub. He then lowered his voice. 'Look, all isn't as it seems. Yes, the company was losing money, but it wasn't down to any downturn in fortunes. Not directly, anyway. Look, you have to believe me when I say that I had nothing to do with Dave's death.'

Hardwick said nothing, but gave Patrick Allen a look which requested that he continue.

'The company had some problems, but not what you might think. Dave was a useless business partner, if you must know. Yeah, in the early days he used to put a lot of money in and helped the company get off the ground, but in recent years he was on the take more than anything. He tried to cover it up, but the fact is that he was nowhere near as shrewd a businessman as he thought he was. Holes that big in a set of company accounts are pretty bloody obvious if you're the one running the company from day to day.'

'What sort of holes?' Hardwick asked.

'Well, more plugs than holes. I'd noticed quite a drop in the profit margins in recent months. Seems that a lot of money was going out to one particular supplier, a new internet marketing company that Dave had hired to try and increase our presence on the web.'

'And presumably there was no noticeable increase in business to offset the costs?'

'Well, no. But there's a jolly good reason for that.'

Hardwick cocked his head to the side slightly. 'Go on.'

'It was Dave who had all the dealings with the company. Said he wanted to get more involved and this new marketing project should be his little baby. Net Marketing Solutions Ltd, they were called. We were paying three grand a month to Net Marketing Solutions at one point and seemed to be getting nothing for it. No increase in business through the website whatsoever. It was at that point that I did a bit of background research on them. True enough, they had a flashy website with details of previous customers, so I decided to phone a few of them and see what their experiences with the company were. I called two: an online gardening tools supplier and a drama consultant, neither of whom had ever heard of Net Marketing Solutions. Well, at this point I started to get a little worried so I went onto the Companies House website and searched for Net Marketing Solutions Ltd. The registered office was a faceless forwarding address in Regent Street, so I downloaded the shareholders' information. Guess who is the sole shareholder of Net Marketing Solutions?'

'Who?' Hardwick asked, humouring the man.

'One Marianne Spencer. Basically, Dave'd been siphoning off tens of thousands of pounds to himself under the umbrella of this marketing company. Turns out he paid two hundred quid to get a flashy website made and twenty quid a month for a forwarding address, but the stupid sod didn't realise his name would be publicly accessible to anyone willing to pay a couple of pounds.'

'Perhaps Mr Spencer wasn't quite so clever after all,' Hardwick said. 'Did you confront him about it?'

'Oh, yes. He claimed that he knew nothing about it.'

'When was this?'

'Blimey, only a few days ago. Last Thursday, I think it was.'

10

'So what's the theory?' Ellis said. 'Charlie Sparks was on the take and knew he'd been found out so decided to top himself? Or that squeaky-clean Patrick Allen decided enough was enough and he'd bump his business partner off?'

'I'm glad you said that, Ellis,' Hardwick said, rubbing his chin. 'There's certainly something more than a little creepy about Patrick Allen. He doesn't strike me as the sort of man who's quite as squeaky-clean as he claims to be.'

'True, but I'm not sure if that equates to being a murderer. After all, surely Marianne Spencer is complicit in this too, seeing as it was her name on the company which was receiving Wellington Pharmaceuticals' cash every month.'

'Ellis, have you ever tried setting up a limited company?'

'Can't say I have, no.'

'It's remarkably easy. Essentially, anyone can set up a company in anyone's name. A lot of company formation agents don't even request proof of ID. There was nothing to stop Charlie Sparks setting up Net Marketing Solutions Ltd in the name of his wife, Marianne Spencer.'

'But surely business correspondence would come addressed to her?'

'That's the beauty of it. Firstly, let's not forget that Net Marketing Solutions was a sham company and would have received very little in the way of business correspondence, seeing as it wasn't technically doing any business whatsoever. Any correspondence which was sent, of course, would have gone to the registered address of the company, which we now know was a fronting address based in London.'

'Ah yes, but fronting addresses are only used to mask an address. I've looked into it. Your mail is then forwarded on to your physical address for a small fee.'

'Incomplete research is the cancer of detective work, Ellis. The tiny, seemingly insignificant gaps only need overlay some vital piece of information and you'll find the holes open up to such an extent that they swallow any useful evidence we once had.'

'What on earth are you on about, Kempston?'

'You're quite correct that fronting address companies forward one's correspondence on, but a good number of these companies allow you to stipulate not only the address to which it is forwarded, but to which name it is addressed.'

'By Jove, that's incredible. So Charlie Sparks could quite happily receive all business correspondence for Net Marketing Solutions Ltd, in his name and at his home address, albeit a few days later, without his wife, the company's sole shareholder, even knowing it existed?'

'Quite. And I'd be willing to bet that all of the company's payments went into a joint bank account which either Charlie Sparks maintained or his wife had forgotten existed, thereby giving him full access to the cash.'

'So what's the next step?'

'Well, I think it would be prudent to pay Marianne Spencer another visit, don't you?'

11

Marianne Spencer looked far more like the expectedly devastated widow that morning than she did on Hardwick's and Flint's previous visit, her eyes red raw from apparent hours of sobbing. The cynic in Hardwick wondered if perhaps the tears were a knee-jerk response to the net which was now closing in on her, but he quickly shook that thought from his mind. *Keep your head clear, Kempston,* he told himself. Latching on to theories too quickly can be dangerous.

The china tea set which rattled on the serving tray as Marianne Spencer trundled into the living room had clearly seen better days. It was either very well used or much neglected. Not a word was said as she carefully poured the swirling tea into each cup before adding a dash of milk and barely showing the spoon to the marbling liquid.

'A lot of people say you should add the hot tea to the milk. Something to do with the milk cooling the tea that hits it rather than the tea burning the poured milk. I've never had any problems doing it this way.'

Ellis Flint decided to ignore all talk of tea and turn instead to the question of Net Marketing Solutions Ltd.

'Have you ever heard of the company, Mrs Spencer?'

Hardwick thought he noted a faint flicker of recognition in Marianne Spencer's eyes.

'No. No, I can't say I have.'

'Only Companies House have you listed as a director.'

'Oh. Well, I don't know. I can only imagine it was one of Dave's businesses. He sometimes asked me to be named as a board member or account holder on certain things.'

'And why would he do that?'

Marianne Spencer looked expectantly at Flint for a few moments.

'Oh, come on. Surely an intelligent man like you can work it out. Dave had a few different financial interests. He did quite well when he was on television a few years ago and invested most of his money wisely, as far as I'm aware. I mean, I was never really one for looking after money. That was always Dave's responsibility. But I'm fully aware that a few of his plans and ideas might not have made the taxman too happy if he'd found out about it. I presume,' she added, 'that we can keep that between us.'

'Quite,' Hardwick responded.

'I mean, I'm sure the police have plenty of other avenues to follow at the moment, what with the suspicious circumstances surrounding my husband's death.'

'Oh, I'm sure they do, Mrs Spencer,' Hardwick said.

'They? Surely you mean we?'

'Do I indeed?'

'Well, you're a police officer, surely.'

'And whatever gave you that idea, Mrs Spencer?' Hardwick replied coyly.

'What? Well, I mean... Well, who are you then? I thought you referred to yourself as a detective.'

'I did. But I didn't once mention the police.'

'Is this legal? What right do you have to barge in and bombard me with a barrage of questions if you're not the police?' Marianne Spencer was starting to become rather agitated.

'We didn't barge in anywhere, Mrs Spencer. You may recall that you invited us into your house, made us a pot of tea — which, I must say, was very nice indeed — and voluntarily entered into a conversation with us regarding your husband's business interests. I don't see what could possibly be construed as illegal, do you, Ellis?' Hardwick turned momentarily to Flint, seeking the high-ground through his rhetorical request for agreement.

'This is impersonation! It's fraud! I'll have nothing more to do with it. Get out of my house!'

12

'Suspicious or predictable?' Ellis Flint asked as they stood morosely at the end of the driveway leading to Manor Farm.

'Suspiciously predictable,' Hardwick replied. 'Some might say predictably suspicious, too. Either way, we need to find out more about Wellington Pharmaceuticals' payments to Net Marketing Solutions. Hand over your phone, Ellis. I'll give Patrick Allen another call.'

'Can't you use your own?'

'My own what?'

'Mobile phone!'

'Don't be so daft, man. Why on earth would I want to carry one of those?'

Ellis Flint said nothing and took his phone from his pocket and handed it to Hardwick, who seemed to be more than a little adept at using what he claimed was an unfamiliar gadget. Within seconds he had the phone to his ear and Flint could hear the faint buzzing of the ringing tone.

'Mr Allen? Kempston Hardwick here. I just wondered if perhaps we might be able to have another quick chat. Yes, I know we left not long ago. Oh, she did? No, I understand. Thank you.'

The call seemingly ended, Hardwick handed the phone back to Ellis Flint.

'Well, that's interesting,' he said, turning his head to look up at the bedroom window of Manor Farm. 'Patrick Allen said that he had only just got off the phone to Marianne Spencer. Immediately after the door was closed to us, she was on the phone to him to warn him that we weren't police officers and that he shouldn't say any more to us.'

'The cheeky mare!' Ellis exclaimed.

'Oh, no, she's well within her rights to do so. After all, we aren't police officers.'

'So what do we do now?'

'A slight change of tack, that's all,' Hardwick said in a staccato voice as Ellis Flint struggled to catch up with his sudden march.

A taxi was hailed back on the high street, and Hardwick instructed the driver to take them to the Bunhill

Industrial Estate, the home of Wellington Pharmaceuticals.

'Are you mad, Kempston? Patrick Allen is already aware that we shouldn't be speaking to him,' Flint cried.

'And we're not. We're going to find someone else to speak to. Someone else who might have access to the company's records without having a vested interest in covering up Charlie Sparks's death.'

On arriving at the premises of Wellington Pharmaceuticals, Hardwick and Flint made their way into the main reception area. Hardwick noted that no-one was currently occupying the reception desk — a fact he decided to take advantage of as he headed towards the lift on the other side of the room.

'Where are you going? We can't just go walking around!' Flint asked nervously.

'Down to the basement, of course.'

'Why the basement?'

'Did you not hear Patrick Allen earlier, man? Honestly, you really must learn to listen. He referred to the accounts department being in the basement.'

'I must admit I didn't pick up on that,' Flint said.

'So I see. The most pertinent points are often those which would otherwise pass you by. Never let anything pass you by, Ellis,' said Hardwick, pressing the down arrow on the lift's outer control panel. As the doors slid open, he beckoned Ellis Flint inside.

Upon reaching the basement, Hardwick and Flint made their way down a short, narrow corridor, the walls of which were adorned with a number of cupboards and cabinets. One open door at the end of the corridor led to the accounts department. The room was well-lit, and contained three desks, one of which seated a young man who looked up as the pair entered.

'Oh, hello. Sorry, I did ask Emma at reception not to allow visitors down here today. Got an awful lot to do.'

'I'm sorry. We'll be brief," Hardwick said. "We've come about the death of one of the company's owners, Dave Spencer. We need to take a look at some records.'

'I see. Do you have any ID on you?'

As Ellis Flint shuffled nervously and started to speak, Hardwick interrupted him. 'Well, despite the company's shortcomings, the security is certainly on top form!' he joked, nudging Ellis to laugh along too.

'Sorry?' the young man said.

'We only had to show it to the young girl on reception not thirty seconds ago.'

'Ah, yes. Sorry, that explains why she let you down here. Just we've been told by Mr Allen that all visitors need to provide ID for the foreseeable future. Something to do with amateurs poking their noses in.'

'Well!' Flint began, Hardwick sensing his offence.

'Well, well, well!' Hardwick said, glaring at Flint. 'Looks like we've got pretenders to the throne, eh? Do you have a description of these amateurs, Mr...?'

'Oh, sorry. Reynolds,' the young man answered, rising to shake Hardwick's hand. 'Billy Reynolds. I look after the accounts and records. As well as most of the computer systems. Company Dogsbody, some might say.'

'I see. So, any description of the people you mentioned?'

'No, afraid not. Just been told to stay vigilant. So, what can I do for you, officers?'

'We want to take a look at the accounts for the past couple of years, if we may. Payments made, in particular.'

'No problem at all. Anything in particular you're looking for?'

Hardwick kept deliberately vague. He didn't want Patrick Allen getting wind of how close he may be to cracking the case.

As they began to rifle through filing cabinets in search of the vital records, Billy Reynolds watched over them for a few minutes, seemingly unsure as to whether or not he should be allowing this and wondering how his boss would react. In acquiescence to authority, though, he retired a few minutes later to the upper floors.

The cupboards, and the files within them, were musty and coated with a thick layer of dust, belying their relatively young age. Computers, Hardwick noted, had a terrible habit of contributing to the never-ending flow of dust around an office. Barely fifteen minutes into their search, Hardwick slammed shut the door of the metal filing cabinet and raised a finger to his chin.

'Nothing. Time for another plan of action.' Hardwick headed towards the computer which sat proud on the desk in the middle of the room and nudged the mouse. A password prompt appeared on the screen.

'Now, come on, Kempston. He didn't say anything about looking through his computer,' Ellis reminded him.

'Nonsense. You keep an eye out on the corridor. Let me know if you see or hear anything.'

Hardwick tapped at the computer's keyboard, after which the password prompt disappeared and the computer's desktop filled the screen. He opened the accounts software and found his way through to the Supplier Payments screen. Filtering the payments by supplier, he very quickly discovered that a vast number of payments indeed had been made to Net Marketing Solutions Ltd over the previous months.

'Eighty-five thousand pounds!' Hardwick exclaimed.

'Sorry?'

'Eighty-five thousand pounds! That's how much Wellington Pharmaceuticals have paid to Net Marketing Solutions Ltd, otherwise known as Marianne Spencer, over the past eighteen months. There's something very strange going on here,' he said, as he closed down the accounts software and re-locked the computer's screen. 'And we're going to have to take some time to work out exactly what.'

'Just one thing, Kempston,' Ellis Flint asked as he followed Hardwick down the corridor. 'How on Earth did you know his password?'

'Well, come on. Billy Reynolds would have had to set a password at some point, and he strikes me as someone who'd be security conscious. Even the best of us take some sort of visual inspiration when thinking of a new password. Did you not see the number of photographs of Diana Dors on his desk?'

'Ah, is that who it was?' Ellis asked, pretending not to have noticed the scantily-clad images.

'Indeed. I knew he wouldn't keep it too simple, so I took an educated guess that Billy Reynolds would have been born around 1982. His password was *diana82*.

'Bloody hell, that's incredible,' Ellis Flint replied.

'Not incredible at all, Ellis. It's human psychology at its simplest level.

* * *

An increasingly-irate Patrick Allen exhaled heavily as he continued to watch the two men leave the premises on his CCTV screen.

13

The soft brown leather snuggled into Hardwick's back as the regal sounds of Wagner's *Der fliegende Hollände* filled his ears and mind. The wisps of smoke from the Montecristo No. 2 danced around his nostrils, completing the almighty sensory experience with which he was so familiar. The familiar song of the helmsman rang through his ears.

...With tempest and storm on distant seas...

Hardwick was pulled back from his realm of numinosity by the shrill ringing of the doorbell.

The appearance of Detective Inspector Rob Warner and Detective Constable Sam Kerrigan was incongruous to Hardwick's relaxed state, and he groaned outwardly as he ushered them into his living room with rolled eyes.

The young DC Kerrigan made a point of circuiting

the room, seemingly looking for some sort of incrimi-
nating evidence as he sauntered about with his hands
thrust into the pockets of his grey suit trousers. DI
Warner, hands likewise situated in the confines of his
pockets, nodded his head in the direction of the gramo-
phone. 'Beethoven?' he asked.

Hardwick simply stared at DI Warner for a few
moments before turning the volume down to an
inaudible level, followed by the utterance of a simple yet
inference-laden 'No'.

'Mr Hardwick, I'll get to the point. We've had some
complaints regarding your interference in the lives of
local citizens.'

'I presume you're referring to my investigating the
murder of Charlie Sparks, Inspector?' Hardwick
enquired innocently.

'I am, yes. I've come to ask you to stop this silly
charade and keep away from the family and friends of
Charlie Sparks.'

'Am I doing anything illegal, Inspector?'

'That all depends,' DI Warner replied, 'on whether
or not your actions could be seen as interfering with the
course of justice.'

'Oh, on the contrary, Inspector. My sole aim is to
achieve justice. Like you, all I want is to see Charlie
Sparks's killer arrested,' Hardwick stated innocuously.

'All the same, that is the job of the police, not of some jumped-up charlatan who thinks he can go one better.' DI Warner spoke with an increasing sense of frustration. DC Kerrigan stood provocatively over his shoulder, smirking in Hardwick's direction. 'Now, I'm going to need your word that you will keep your nose out of business that doesn't concern you.'

'Will you now, Inspector?'

'I will. Do I have your word?'

'I'm afraid not. I don't see that my actions are against the law, nor do I see any reason for me to stop trying to help you find a cold-blooded killer.'

'In that case, I'm going to have to place you under arrest for the intent to pervert the course of justice. Maybe a night or two in a cold prison cell will change your mind.'

As DC Kerrigan took great pleasure in reading him his rights, Hardwick felt his teeth grating; not at his arrest, but at the Inspector's use of the word "prison" in favour of Hardwick's preferred "gaol".

* * *

The atmosphere at the gaol was as Hardwick had expected: dank and miserable. In order to pass the time, Hardwick found himself running through the stanzas of

Oscar Wilde's *Ballad of Reading Gaol* in his mind, perhaps in a private display of self-indulgence.

And all the woe that moved him so
　That he gave that bitter cry,
　And the wild regrets and the bloody sweats
　None knew so well as I:
　For he who lives more lives than one
　More deaths than one must die.

He had reached the penultimate stanza when the door to his cell unbolted loudly; ironically, he thought, at the line "In silence let him lie".

'Visitor,' the moustachioed police sergeant said, stepping aside to usher Ellis Flint into the cell. Hardwick said nothing.

'Hello, Kempston.' Ellis waited for a reply but none was forthcoming. 'I've paid your bail. They tell me you can leave now. Probably best if we leave the investigation alone, though, eh?' He thought he could see the disappointment marked on Hardwick's face. 'I mean, I'm not one for giving up on a challenge either, but I think it's probably for the best in this case.'

'Ellis, are you familiar with The Ballad of Reading Gaol?'

'Read it at school once, I think. Why?' he replied.

'And all men kill the thing they love, / By all let this be heard, / Some do it with a bitter look, / Some with a flattering word, / The coward does it with a kiss, / The brave man with a sword!'

'Now, if I know you, Kempston, you're trying to draw some parallels here. Are you saying that Charlie Sparks was the coward?'

'In this sense, perhaps. But that's not the real question. The real question is: who was the brave man, and what was the sword?'

* * *

Hardwick collected his possessions from the desk sergeant and began to make his way towards the exit when he heard the clicking of a door latch and the familiar voice of Detective Inspector Rob Warner.

'Ah, Mr Hardwick. I trust you enjoyed the pleasure of our hospitality.'

'Very much so. Although I can't say much for the receptionist,' he remarked, nodding in the direction of the large, moustachioed desk sergeant.

'We'll see what we can do. Sign our guest book on the way out?' the Inspector replied.

Hardwick made no comment and turned to head for the exit.

'Oh, and Hardwick? Thought you might like to know: the autopsy report is in. Charlie Sparks died from poisoning. I'll be making a full statement to the press later today.'

'Very good,' Hardwick replied. 'While you're at it, you might want to let them know that JFK is dead and the wheel has been invented.'

14

By the time Hardwick had returned home, his mind was full of noise and confusion. As he scrunched the pillows in tightly to his head, the developing quiet was pierced by the ringing of the telephone. Grumbling to himself, he leant over and picked up the receiver.

'Hardwick.'

'Hello, it's Patrick Allen here. Listen, I need to see you.'

'Right, well I'll pop over first thing tomorrow morning, Mr Allen.'

'No, I need to see you now. Alone. Meet me at the office in twenty minutes.'

Before Hardwick had a chance to protest, the line had gone dead. Sighing over-audibly to no-one available to hear, he sat up, rubbed his forehead and headed downstairs. Swapping his tartan slippers for patent leather Oxfords, he donned his coat and headed out.

* * *

The welcome Hardwick received from Patrick Allen was expectedly cold. He was ushered upstairs into the private office, whereupon Patrick Allen sauntered over to the mahogany drinks cabinet.

'Whisky?' Allen asked.

'Not for me, thanks.'

'Anything at all?'

'Campari, if you have it,' Hardwick said, knowing full well that he didn't, having surveyed the drinks table on his way in. Accepting a drink from a murder suspect who owned a company which sold poisons wasn't top of Hardwick's list of priorities for that day.

'I'm afraid I don't. Don't often see it around much these days. Mind if I have a dram?'

'Please do,' Hardwick replied.

Patrick Allen took his large glass of scotch and sat down in the plush chair behind his desk. Crossing his legs, he clasped his hands over his knee and looked only at the whisky glass on the desk in front of him.

'You see, I have to ask you something. I know you've spent some time in here looking through our records.

And I also know you're not a police officer. I'm not entirely sure who you are at all, if I'm honest, but all I know is that you're not welcome here.' It was at this point that Patrick Allen's eyes first met Hardwick's.

'Mr Allen, I'm simply—'

'The fact of the matter is, what you want is not here. You have all the information you need, I can assure you.'

'I don't dispute that for one minute, Mr Allen. I quite believe that I have all the information. My job now is to work out exactly what it means.'

'I can tell you exactly what it means,' Patrick Allen said, leaning forward slightly. 'But in return I want your word that you will not set foot on these premises again.'

'My word?'

'You seem to be an honest man, Mr Hardwick. Your word will be good enough for me.'

Hardwick made no commitment. 'What do you have for me, Mr Allen?'

Patrick Allen sighed and sat back in his chair, taking his whisky glass with him.

'The payments to Net Marketing Solutions. You're quite right. It's Marianne's company.'

'And you sanctioned these payments?'

'In a way, yes.'

'Why?'

'Oh, come on, man. You've spoken to Marianne. She

must have given you some indication. Dave Spencer had been playing around, all right? Had a bit on the side and Marianne found out about her. Well, that was the last straw for her. As far as she was concerned, her marriage was over, and she went about finding her own "other man". She asked me if there was any way Dave's share of the company's money could somehow find its way to her. He'd left her with nothing, so she had no escape. The mortgage and bills were put in her name, so she had nowhere to go. I suggested setting up Net Marketing Solutions to take payments from Wellington Pharma-ceuticals.'

Hardwick thought for a moment. 'You say she found her own "other man'. Were you and Marianne Spencer close, Mr Allen?'

Patrick Allen thought about his words for a moment. 'Sometimes, a woman needs reliable male company. Sometimes she needs to feel loved and cherished. Mari-anne and I are good friends.'

'And Dave Spencer's mistress? Who was she?'

'Some young tart. A stripper or something. Roxanne de la Rue, I think her name was. Works in a club down in Soho. The Vines.'

Hardwick made a mental note. 'What can you tell me about the relationship between Dave Spencer and Roxanne de la Rue, Mr Allen?'

'Nothing more than I already have, I'm afraid. Marianne confided in me about it and said she had suspected something for a long time, but I'm really not able to tell you any more than that.'

'And if I were to pay her a visit? Do you think she might reveal anything which might help us to find Dave Spencer's killer?'

'I should imagine she wouldn't be backwards in coming forward, if you see what I mean.'

Hardwick raised an eyebrow.

'She's a pretty... open... person, from what I hear. If you catch my drift. You'll probably end up getting a few more details than you bargained for.'

With that thought foremost in his mind, Hardwick bade Patrick Allen farewell and left the premises of Wellington Pharmaceuticals before heading for the nearest public phone box. Sliding himself into the booth, he lifted the Bakelite handset and dialled the eleven digits, his other hand hovering a twenty-pence piece over the coin slot. The familiar click of the placed call was followed by the dulcet tones of Ellis Flint answering.

'Ah, Ellis. Hardwick here. Looks as though we might have to take a trip down to Soho.'

'Soho? When?'

'Tonight. Meet me at the station in ten minutes.'

'What, now? It's ten-thirty at night!'

'Where we're going, that's probably a good thing.'

* * *

Neither Hardwick nor Ellis Flint said much at all during the early stages of the train journey. As the train rolled past Kentish Town and approached its London terminus, however, Ellis Flint could resist no longer and looked up at Hardwick, sat opposite him, and pushed his newspaper gently downward to force him to meet his gaze.

'Now, what's all this about? Where are we going, exactly?'

'I told you. Soho.' Hardwick broke Ellis Flint's gaze and lifted the newspaper back up.

'Yes, but where? And why?'

'We have to see a young lady about something. Something which might help us find Dave Spencer's killer.'

Hardwick's voluminous use of the final word had Ellis Flint twisting round in his seat, ensuring that no other passenger in the carriage had overheard.

'Do calm down, Ellis. We are the only people in this carriage,' Hardwick remarked, sensing Flint's unease.

'How on Earth would you know that? You've not

taken your nose out of that newspaper since I met you at the station!'

'Observation is everything, my dear man. And it need not be done through one's eyes.'

Ellis Flint gazed at Hardwick for a few moments before rendering any further conversation futile and diverting his attention to that evening's copy of the London Evening Standard which rested on the seat beside him.

The tube connection to Leicester Square was completed by way of the Piccadilly line, a line which Hardwick had declared to Ellis Flint to be a favourite of his in a rare expression of opinion and sentiment. 'Any line which contains Covent Garden, Piccadilly Circus and Knightsbridge is a joy to behold,' he had declared, as they alighted the train at Leicester Square. The short walk up the vibrant Charing Cross Road had the pair slalom through tourists and pedestrians, Hardwick racing on ahead of the lumbering Ellis Flint, who could only watch with amazement and amusement as Hardwick continued to drop his shoulders, arch his back and side-step every obstruction in his path. The way the man moved was almost comical at the best of times, but his trademark regimented gait seemed vastly loosened on the meandering walk up the Charing Cross Road.

A swift left-turn took them over the pedestrian

crossing and briefly onto Shaftesbury Avenue before crossing the road to head up Greek Street, home to The Vines.

'Where are we going, Kempston? Is it much further?'

'Not at all. In fact, we're here.'

'Here?' Ellis Flint asked, looking only at Hardwick.

'Or, more specifically, there,' Hardwick said, pointing up at the sign above the neon-red door which stood proudly at the side of the pavement.

'The Vines? But surely that's a... well, you know...'

'I'm reliably informed so, yes.'

'Hardwick, you dirty old bugger, you!'

Nodding pleasant greetings to the doorman, Hardwick entered through the door which had been held open for him, closely followed by Ellis Flint.

The door opened onto a flight of stairs, similarly lit by sensuous red lighting. The wooden staircase descended some ten or eleven steps before turning ninety degrees to the left for a further seven or eight steps, thus opening onto a vast expanse of tables and sofas. An illuminated bar stood to one side of the room. A number of shiny metal poles connected the tables to the ceiling, some of them adorned by women wearing not very much at all.

Hardwick approached the bar and ordered drinks for both Ellis and himself. The barman was a tall,

Mediterranean-looking man, a man who had a permanent quarter-smile, but never more or less. The short dark curls on his head looked well greased, and he spoke with a slight foreign accent. Immediately after ordering the drinks Hardwick enquired as to the whereabouts of Roxanne de la Rue. The barman said nothing, but just pointed at the woman gyrating on the pole towards the back of the room. One man sat on his own at the table, sipping on his drink as he gawked up at her. Hardwick signalled to Ellis Flint and they approached the table.

As the two men sat on the uncomfortable wooden seats, the man who had been sat alone at the table seemed uneasy and stood up to leave. The dancer, now known to Hardwick and Flint as Roxanne de la Rue, began gyrating in their direction.

'Excuse me, Miss. May we ask you a few questions?' Hardwick asked.

'You can ask me whatever you like, sweetie,' the woman said, unclasping her brassiere and flinging it at Hardwick.

'Now, that's not necessary, thank you. We just want to ask you a few things.'

'Like what, hot lips?' she said, as she leant provocatively over Hardwick, her voluptuous bosom dangling in his face.

'Like your relationship with Charlie Sparks, Miss de

la Rue,' Hardwick said, wishing to hurry the conversation on to less sexual matters. Immediately, the dancer's entire body language changed. She stared at Hardwick and Flint for a few moments before climbing down from the table, retrieving her brassiere from the floor and telling them that they should follow her.

Hardwick and Flint followed Roxanne de la Rue into the back rooms of the club; a corridor off of which a number of curtained booths were situated. Another scantily-clad woman walked towards them. 'Got yourself two for the price of one there, Roxy!' she suggested, before carrying on her giggling journey. Ellis Flint looked thoroughly embarrassed; Hardwick indifferent.

'Better hope my wife doesn't get wind that I've been down here,' Ellis said quietly to Hardwick.

'I don't imagine for one minute she tends to move in these circles, Ellis.'

'Most men aren't keen on the idea. One of the reasons I've never been married,' Roxanne de la Rue shouted over her shoulder.

She drew back the curtain as she ushered Hardwick and Flint into one of the vacated side booths. Aside from a small table with a large bowl of cash situated on top of it, a sofa was all that was inside the booth; bright red and shaped like a pair of voluminous lips.

'Now, you better make this quick as I'm losing

money every minute I'm in here,' Roxanne de la Rue stated. She sat down on the sofa and Hardwick signalled for an evermore embarrassed-looking Ellis Flint to sit down next to her. Flint's body language signified unease: his legs crossed away from Roxanne de la Rue, his eyes flitting from side to side. Hardwick began to pace back and forth across the room.

'Now, what exactly was the nature of your relationship with Dave Spencer?'

'Was? What do you mean "was"?' she replied.

'I mean Dave Spencer collapsed and died on Friday night while performing at a pub near where he lived.'

'Died? Oh God. What? How?'

'That's what we're trying to find out. We heard from one of his colleagues that he may have entered into a relationship with you recently.'

'Well, I dunno about relationship. I mean, I get pretty close to a lot of guys who come in here. Nature of the job, really, innit?'

Hardwick noted that Roxanne de la Rue seemed to be more than a little short of natural human emotion.

'I should imagine so. How would you describe your relationship with Dave Spencer?' Hardwick asked.

'Profitable,' she replied, honestly and simply.

'Profitable?'

'Well, let's just say certain things earn more money

than others in here. There's a reason there are separate rooms, Inspector.'

Ellis Flint interjected. 'Oh, we're not–' before Hardwick interrupted him.

'So your relationship was purely...'

'Sexual, yes. In my eyes it wasn't even that. It was business. Listen, Dave Spencer was like any other guy who comes in here. They think they've got something special with you and you have to let them believe that. Keeps them coming, if you'll pardon the pun.' Ellis Flint tittered, but the joke was largely lost on Hardwick.

'What made Dave Spencer think he had something special with you?' Hardwick asked. 'Surely if his only contact with you was in a strip club, that keeps business and pleasure separate,' Hardwick suggested.

'Inspector, this is exactly the sort of place that mixes business and pleasure very nicely, if you catch my drift. Besides, we didn't always conduct "business" in the club. That's not to be repeated, mind,' she said, leaning in towards Hardwick. 'I could lose my job if that gets out.'

'You mean you charged Dave Spencer for sex outside of the club?'

'I never charged him for nothing outside of here, Inspector. Thing is, he was a regular customer. Used to pay well. If he rang up and asked me to meet him for a drink or come out to dinner with him, who am I to say no? Suppliers and customers entertain each other all the time in any other line of work. What's wrong with me getting a few free meals and drinks and the promise of more business?'

'The problem is that Dave Spencer might not have quite seen it like that,' Ellis Flint remarked.

'Well, that's his stupid fault, innit?'

'Miss de la Rue,' Hardwick said. 'I'm not quite sure I believe your version of events. We have it on good authority that you've been conducting a relationship with Dave Spencer for quite some time. Up until his death, that is.'

Roxanne de la Rue said nothing.

'Miss de la Rue, were you engaged to Dave Spencer?' Hardwick asked directly. Roxanne looked up sharply at Hardwick, her eyes revealing the whole truth.

Finally, she spoke. 'Who have you been speaking to?'

'No-one.'

'Well there's no way you could possibly know that,' she said, her interest clearly piqued.

'Oh, there is. I can see from here that you have recently worn a thin ring on your fourth left finger for a quite considerable period of time. The mark which is still visible shows that you very rarely took it off, thereby suggesting a wedding or engagement ring. We already know you're not married, so that leaves only one possibility. The fact that you're now no longer wearing it suggests a recently-ended engagement; one which didn't end on the best of terms, judging by the small lacerations you made trying to wrench the thing off.'

Ellis Flint cocked his head in amazement at Hardwick.

'And there's me thinking you were readin' me bloody mind,' Roxanne de la Rue said, settling back into the sofa. 'Right. Well, seeing as you're so cock-sure, why don't you tell me what happened, Inspector?'

'That's what we're here to find out, Miss de la Rue. Whichever way you look at it, Dave Spencer is dead and we need to find out every last detail about his life in order to find his killer. You do want us to find his killer, don't you?'

'Of course I bloody do!' the woman exclaimed as she began to break down into tears. 'Listen, Dave and I might have gone our separate ways recently, but I still love him and want to know what happened to him.' Her voice under pressure betrayed what now appeared to be her cockney persona, a far more refined accent cutting through the tears and sobs. 'Don't get me wrong, I hate him too. He promised me for months that we would get married. He even bought me an engagement ring.'

'Did you know he was already married?'

'Yes, of course I did. He told me his marriage was on

the rocks and that he was sorting out the details before he and I would be together. For good. We'd talked about our future together. We were going to be so happy.'

'Miss de la Rue, if you don't mind me saying so, it sounds like a rather odd relationship.'

'All sorts of different people fall in love, Inspector. You must know that.'

'I'm afraid love isn't near the top of my list of priorities, Miss de la Rue. Tell me, what exactly did you see in Dave Spencer?'

Roxanne de la Rue looked towards the floor. Hardwick glanced over at the bowl full of cash and back at Roxanne.

* * *

'Goodnight, gents,' the doorman said as Hardwick and Flint exited the club and made their way back down Greek Street.

'So she just wanted him for his money?' Ellis Flint asked.

'Predictably so, yes. I had suspected as much.'

'He'd promised her marriage, she'd seen the pound signs, and then it all went belly up. So what, she killed him?'

'It's not to be ruled out, but somehow I can't quite see

it. There are thousands of women in the world who attempt to marry for money, and thousands more who have their hearts broken. That doesn't necessarily turn them into killers.'

'Well,' Ellis Flint said, 'You've got to be pretty disjointed to have a job like that, haven't you? I mean, perhaps Charlie Sparks's money was going to be her escape route out of there. At worst, maybe she did really love him and couldn't bear to be without him. It's hardly a new concept, Kempston. Even Romeo and Juliet met their fate because their love wasn't meant to be.'

Hardwick stopped in his tracks and stared at Ellis Flint. 'I hardly think Charlie Sparks and Roxanne de la Rue are comparable to Romeo and Juliet, do you?'

'True. More Ronald and Janet, I suppose.' Ellis Flint glanced at Hardwick for any sign of his recognition of the joke, but saw none. 'Anyway, there's something not quite right about her. She's clearly a bloody good actor – you saw the way she flitted from a cheap cockney persona back to her real personality. What's to stop her being able to cover over a murder?'

'No, I think the suspicion swings back the other way, if anything.'

'How do you mean?' Ellis asked.

'Well, logically it seems that Marianne Spencer will have caught wind of her husband's philandering with

Miss de la Rue and been somewhat angry, don't you think?'

'I think that'd probably describe it, yes.'

'In which case, the hatchet of suspicion now sways above her head. No, I think there's something not quite right about the Spencers' marriage. I'm almost sure that will provide the key to unravelling what went on at the Freemason's Arms that night.'

Ellis Flint chuckled slightly as he spoke. 'Well, it's a blasted shame that Marianne Spencer won't let us within a hundred yards of her house then, isn't it?'

'Since someone let slip that we weren't police officers, yes,' Hardwick said accusingly.

'Now steady on, old boy. In fact, I–' Ellis Flint's protestations were halted by Hardwick's continuing monologue.

'But I don't suppose that should matter too much. In my experience, the interview process is the weakest point of the investigation. I mean, what have we actually discovered through speaking to people? That Charlie Sparks had a mistress in London? That his wife was on the take from a company he ran with an old school friend? Ellis, there are deep and dark secrets in every single life. We all have skeletons in our cupboards, but what we've found out so far doesn't even constitute a pile of bones. No, there's definitely more to this than meets the eye. I say we should head to the Spencer house and see what we can dig up.'

'For Christ's sake, Kempston, didn't you listen to a word I said? If we set foot anywhere near Marianne Spencer, she'll call the police on us!'

'I didn't mention anything about going near Marianne Spencer,' Hardwick replied innocently.

15

The bracken rustled as two branches parted to reveal the impassioned face of Kempston Hardwick as he observed the Mercedes rumbling away from Manor Farm (which still wasn't a farm), one Marianne Spencer occupying the controls. A small tortoiseshell cat mewed its discontent at having been ejected from its lair some minutes earlier.

'Been quite some time since I spent my days making dens in bushes, Kempston.'

'Nonsense. I bet you were quite the reconnaissance man in the Army,' Hardwick replied, with his tongue slightly in his cheek.

'Well, not exactly, no.'

'How long were you in the Army for, exactly, Ellis?'

Ellis Flint ignored the question. 'Say, I bet you were

the sort of child who used to make dens and tree-houses as well.'

'I was never one for practicalities, Ellis. Besides, one can make oneself practically invisible anywhere one wishes, if one knows the right ways.'

'So why have we just spent the past ten minutes crouched in a bush, staving off cramp?'

'You struck me as the "sort of child" who'd make dens. I thought you might like to revisit the good old days,' Hardwick said, in such a way that Ellis Flint could have no idea as to whether he was being sarcastic, facetious or plain honest.

'So, how do you propose we get in, exactly?'

'Quite simple, really. Did you notice that Marianne Spencer left the property by way of the side gate?'

'Well, yes.'

'In which case, one can presume one of two things. Either she intends to re-enter the property by way of the side gate, meaning that it'll be easily opened — have you ever seen a lock on a side gate? We certainly didn't see her locking this one. Or that it only locks from the inside, in which case it won't be locked at all.'

'Well, let's just hope she's left her signed confession note in the back garden, then,' Ellis Flint remarked sarcastically. The comment went either unheard or ignored by Hardwick.

'Ah-ha, almost right,' Hardwick said, as he reached the wooden side gate. 'There's a catch on the inside, but the Spencers often operate it from the outside, it seems. Can you see the length of green twine sticking out between the fence panels there? I'd be willing to bet that the other end is tied to the gate's latch on the inside.' With that, Hardwick tugged the stiff twine, observing the metallic clunk of the latch lifting on the inside of the gate as the door shifted an inch or so. 'Not the most security-conscious way of locking one's gate, but I'm hardly complaining in this instance.'

Hardwick and Flint followed the path round towards the back garden, treading carefully and evenly on the flagstones which were set within the gravel path. Despite gravel being perfectly suitable for walking on in any other circumstance, it struck Hardwick as rather odd that the presence of flagstones meant that the gravel was almost never walked on.

On reaching the back garden, Hardwick surveyed the scene. Glancing up at the first floor, he groaned loudly as he noticed the open bathroom window.

'Surely that's a good thing?' Ellis asked.

'It certainly helps, but it does nothing to provide a challenge, does it?'

'Oh, I don't know. Watching you shimmy up the drainpipe should provide some entertainment.'

And entertaining it was, as a route consisting of water butts, drainpipes and window-sills led the pair slowly but surely to the Spencers' bathroom window. Although he attempted to climb through the window with the grace of Hardwick, Ellis Flint did find himself in something of a tighter situation, his build being far from fat but still unavoidably stockier than the slim frame of Kempston Hardwick.

From the bathroom, the pair stepped lightly across the cream carpet towards the front of the house — the usual location of the master bedroom in most traditional British homes.

'What are we actually looking for?' Ellis Flint asked.

'I'm not entirely sure. Files of some sort. Something concrete which could help give us some sort of direction. Something that is a little more than just plain odd.'

The door to the master bedroom creaked slightly as it was opened, leaving Ellis Flint frozen to the spot. After being reminded by Hardwick that Marianne Spencer, now the sole tenant of Manor Farm, had left by car some minutes earlier, he regained his composure and entered the bedroom.

A large wooden-framed bed stood proud from the far wall, its light dressing adorned with two plush red cushions and a small ragged teddy bear. An old framed-photograph of Charlie Sparks bowing slightly to meet Her Majesty the Queen was hung on the wall above the headboard. The gilt caption-plate showed the date and location as the 1981 Royal Variety Performance at the Theatre Royal. Hardwick doubted very much if Her Majesty would have actually enjoyed Charlie Sparks's act all that much. He pondered that she must actually get quite exasperated with much of the abysmal tripe she was subjected to on such occasions, always being obliged to tell the performers how much she had enjoyed their act, whilst quietly dying a little inside. Hardwick was pleased to be a man who told things exactly as he saw them. No false frontage, no lying to oneself, no dying a little inside. Not that he ever knew any other way, that is.

The bedroom struck Hardwick and Flint as being remarkably normal; the en-suite bathroom leading off to the right and a sweeping arc of wardrobes joining the en-suite to the main bedroom door. Hardwick was immediately attracted to the wardrobes, looking as he did for anywhere that files might be kept.

'Kempston. There's a safe at the bottom of this one,' Ellis Flint exclaimed, lifting a menagerie of sparkling dresses and blouses to reveal a dark grey metallic box, its frontage empanelled with a black plastic panel, revealing a selection of numbers with two additional buttons labelled "Complete" and "Cancel". 'Looks as though we'll need a combination. Bloody hard luck.'

'Not at all. We've already seen how security conscious the Spencers are. What's the betting that the combination is easy to remember as well? It's a Burlington SecureSafe, which, if I'm not mistaken, requires only a four-digit security code. Tell me, Ellis, what is the first four-digit number you think of?'

'Well, my year of birth, I suppose.'

'Quite. Now, that's a little too obvious, even for the Spencers. What would you look at next?'

'Children's birth years?'

'Indeed. Now, we know the Spencers didn't, or couldn't, have children, so that's ruled out. No, I have a funny feeling that we're looking at both years of birth here. According to the newspaper reports, Dave Spencer was born in 1955, and Marianne in 1958, correct?'

'So I believe, yes.'

Hardwick punched 5-5-5-8 into the safe's keypad, followed by the "Complete" button. No noise was audible, but a tug on the plastic handle revealed the safe to be very much open.

'The rule is, Ellis, if it's easy for you to remember, it's easy for someone else to guess.'

'And you're not mistaken when you refer to yourself

as "someone else", Kempston. I've never seen anything like it!'

'Human psychology is remarkably simple and predictable. That's why it is, in essence, so incredibly boring.'

The safe itself contained very little in the way of obviously valuable pieces. No cash or jewellery was contained within it; only envelopes and documents. Hardwick rifled through the slabs of paper, revealing performance contracts in the name of Dave Spencer, as well as his driving licence counterpart, birth certificate and various other documents.

'Nothing at all in the name of Marianne Spencer,' Ellis Flint noted, as Hardwick murmured in agreement.

'Ah-ha. The Last Will and Testament of Mr David Francis Spencer.'

'Now, Kempston, we can't go reading the man's wi—' Ellis found his words cut off again, this time by the sound of Hardwick's index finger ripping the seal from the envelope. He unfolded the paper concealed within and began to read.

'Looks pretty short to me,' Ellis noted.

'Indeed it is. Primarily because he's left everything to one person.'

'Marianne, presumably.'

'Oh no. He wouldn't have needed to write a will in that case, as his estate would pass to her as his next of kin regardless. This completely changes everything, Ellis. Charlie Sparks left his entire estate to Roxanne de la Rue.'

16

The Fox and Bugle was a heavily-extended thatched pub which sat on the cross-roads in the centre of Fettle-sham. The low ceilings proved to be a challenge for Hardwick, who meandered towards the bar via the path of least resistance.

The pub was decorated with all manner of Italian-style trinkets, the walls adorned with pictures and photographs which seemed to have no relationship to each other, yet appeared to fit perfectly within the surroundings. Hardwick sat himself down on a sofa near the front window and watched the cars passing, stopping occasionally in acquiescence to the pedestrian crossing a few yards further up the road. Ellis Flint returned a few moments later with two drinks and wasted no time in getting straight to the point.

'What's next?' he asked.

'There's no rush, Ellis,' Hardwick replied.

'How can you say that? For all we know, the killer might be out to strike again!'

'Oh, I very much doubt that. No, I think we can quite safely say that the murder of Charlie Sparks was a one-off. I don't imagine for one minute that we're looking at the work of a serial killer. No, we need to assimilate our information and formulate some sort of plan for moving forward.'

'And how do you suggest we do that?' Ellis said.

Hardwick could sense Ellis Flint's growing frustration. 'Well, let's look at what we know so far. Charlie Sparks was poisoned, that much is almost certain. Judging by the symptoms, I'd say we're looking at a very hefty dose of tetanus.'

'Only problem with that is that Charlie Sparks didn't have a mark on him, if you believe the newspaper reports.' Ellis replied.

'Indeed. That's a stumbling block. Either way, he was poisoned and he died. For now, I don't suppose the specific method matters all too much if we can find someone with the means, motive and opportunity to kill Charlie Sparks.'

'Could the killer not have used a hit-man?'

'Come along, Ellis. A poisoning in a pub full of

people? Hardly the mark of the fly-by-night hit-man, is it? No, I think we can discount that. The problem we have is that none of our main suspects were actually at the pub on the night of the murder.'

'What about the landlord, Doug Lilley?' Ellis asked.

'No motive,' came Hardwick's reply.

'He could have been paid to do it.'

'Oh, really, Ellis. Doug Lilley is a career publican. Are you really suggesting that he'd commit the murder of someone he didn't even know in his own pub and risk his entire business and career at the same time? No, I'm sure it must be one of our main suspects. If we're looking at poisoning, the murderer need not have actually been present at the time of death. Particularly with tetanus, one would expect a slow onset of symptoms leading to eventual death.'

'Charlie Sparks's death was nothing like slow and eventual,' Ellis offered. 'The man practically keeled over and died.'

'That's the problem,' Hardwick responded. 'A dose that heavy must have been administered pretty shortly before he went on stage.'

'So what, our killer somehow got into Charlie Sparks's dressing room and had a conversation with him, somehow managing to slip poison into his drink?'

'It's looking entirely possible.'

'But who?' Ellis asked.

'That's the eternal question, Ellis. The only witness is a dead man.'

Ellis Flint sat quietly for a few minutes, feeling really rather despondent. 'But what about the means and motive? Surely we have plenty of leads on those fronts.'

'Oh, indeed we do. The means of obtaining a deadly tetanus cocktail would be extremely easy for someone who ran, say, a pharmaceuticals company.'

'Patrick Allen?' Ellis asked.

'Indeed. Of course, Marianne Spencer had a couple of pretty close ties with Wellington Pharmaceuticals. Her husband was part-owner of the company, for a start, and her love affair with Patrick Allen gives her even more opportunity to obtain chemicals and poisons. I think we can quite safely assume that she also had the means to kill him.'

'That's what I don't understand,' Ellis said. 'Why, if Patrick Allen was having an affair with Marianne Spencer, would he reveal the information about her being the director of Net Marketing Solutions?'

'Quite simple, really. The net's closing in, Ellis. Guilty people do strange things. I shouldn't imagine for one moment that Patrick Allen would think twice about jeopardising a fling in order to save his own skin. Besides, that information would all be publicly available.

Keeping it from us would only make us even more suspicious of him. The problem is that both Patrick Allen and Marianne Spencer also have pretty strong motives. Wellington Pharmaceuticals had been haemorrhaging money and Patrick Allen may have believed at that stage that he'd stand to gain. At least, he'd gain by default by losing a dead weight. And if we're to believe the stories of Charlie Sparks's philandering ways, it's no surprise that his wife would have wanted rid of him.'

'Surely that'd be pretty hypocritical, though, seeing as she was having an affair at the same time.'

'Women are a strange species, Ellis,' Hardwick said. 'Never put anything past them.'

'Including Roxanne de la Rue?'

'Especially Roxanne de la Rue. I'm not entirely sure I'm convinced of the "jilted lover" scenario; there has to be something she's not telling us. As for the means of murdering Charlie Sparks, that's going to take some working out. She did, however, stand to gain more than anyone else from his death. Amassing his entire fortune and future royalties would set her up for life quite nicely.'

'But why?' Ellis Flint exclaimed. 'Why on earth would he have left his entire estate to her if, as she claims, he had led her on with false promises of marriage before leaving her altogether? Surely if he didn't want to be with her, there's no way he'd leave everything he had to her.'

'Unless, of course, he didn't leave her at all,' Hardwick mused.

'But why would Roxanne de la Rue say that he did? What would she have to gain? Surely that would only increase the level of suspicion on her, seeing as it gives her a motive for killing Charlie Sparks.'

'Does it, though? Think about it, Ellis. It's far less likely that the end of a fling would cause someone to commit murder than the revelation of a potentially huge windfall from being the sole beneficiary of his Will. What it actually does is shift our perception of her motive to something far more fatuous and unlikely. When, in actual fact, her motive was to obtain Charlie Sparks's entire estate, which she knew she would receive upon his death.'

'Kempston, why do I get the feeling you're about to drag me into another strip club?'

* * *

'You make out like you don't enjoy it,' Hardwick shouted back to a trailing Ellis Flint as he marched his way up Greek Street for the second time that week.

'Well it's never been my idea to come in here. I don't

see what's wrong with calling her and meeting her at a neutral location.'

'Have you ever tried hunting bears at sea, Ellis? No, we need to speak to her where she feels most comfortable; where she's most likely to reveal her inner thoughts. If her guard is down, we're infinitely more likely to discover the truth.'

The man on the door gave the pair a knowing grin, seemingly recognising them from their previous visit. Ellis Flint returned a coy smile, as if begrudgingly entertaining his partner's whims. Roxanne de la Rue was seated on a rounded stool at the bar as Hardwick and Flint entered The Vines. She seemed to recognise them immediately, but showed little willingness to greet them enthusiastically.

'Miss de la Rue. How nice to see you again,' Hardwick remarked.

'You know, Inspector, there's only so many free visits I can allow you.'

'Oh, we're not here to visit, as such. We're here to ask you a few questions.'

'I told you everything I know the other day, Inspector. I have nothing else to tell you.'

Hardwick shuffled slightly as he deliberated as to when to play his trump card. 'Well, that's not entirely true, is it? I mean, you told us something, but I'm not entirely sure you told us everything. In fact, I've a funny feeling that you didn't actually tell us anything.'

'I've no idea what you mean,' she replied, taking her eyes from the pair and starting to stir her drink.

'You told us that Dave Spencer had promised you marriage and that you had since gone your separate ways as he wasn't as committed to you as he had claimed.'

'That's right.'

'So why, Miss de la Rue, did he see fit to commission a will in which he left his entire estate to you?' Roxanne de la Rue looked visibly taken aback. 'Oh, you're a fine actress, Miss de la Rue. You're a woman whose entire life revolves around duality. Your job is to be something you're not; to entertain and mislead; to elicit certain emotions. I must admit it almost worked with me, too. You had me believing that you were simply a lover scorned and that you had no real motive to kill Charlie Sparks. In fact, you had used your fantastic acting skills to ensure that he gradually fell in love with you until such a time as you were named as the sole beneficiary in his Will, at which point you somehow kill him off and claim the money.'

'That's not true at all!' Roxanne de la Rue protested. 'I loved Dave, but he didn't love me. That's the absolute truth. You have to believe me!'

Hardwick looked sideways at Ellis Flint. 'And why

should we believe you, Miss de la Rue? Whether you're being honest or not, you had a solid motive for killing him. Where were you on the night Charlie Sparks died?'

'Where do you think? The same place I am every bloody night. I was here, at work.'

'Do you have an alibi?' Ellis Flint asked.

'Will the entire staff roster and about eighty sweaty old men do?'

* * *

Hardwick and Flint headed out of Greek Street and back down the Charing Cross Road towards Covent Garden before heading into The Harp. The room upstairs was accessed by a traditional wooden-boarded staircase at the back of the pub, and was ornately decorated and had the look and feel of an Edwardian drawing room, with four small tables and sets of chairs dotted around comfortably. Hardwick and Flint sat at the table nearest the window.

'The problem is,' Flint began, 'Every single suspect has a cast-iron alibi. Marianne Spencer, Patrick Allen and Don Preston were all at home and have had their alibis confirmed by witnesses, and Roxanne de la Rue was at work all night.'

'Indeed, but I wouldn't suppose for one minute that

it puts them all in the clear. There's something that doesn't quite add up.'

Hardwick and Flint both stared out of the window for a good couple of minutes, neither saying a word. It was Ellis Flint who deigned to rekindle the conversation.

'Well, I'm going to get another drink. What's that you've got?'

'Campari,' Hardwick replied, proffering the glass politely to Flint.

'Oh no, thank you. Far too bitter for me.'

The bottom of Hardwick's glass hit the table. 'My God, that's it! We've got it!' Hardwick exclaimed, rising from his chair and dashing towards the staircase leading back down to the main bar.

'Got what? Kempston!' Ellis Flint gulped down three last mouthfuls of his beer and followed Hardwick as quickly as possible. They were back on the Charing Cross Road before he had managed to catch up with him. 'What is it, Kempston?'

'Too bitter, Ellis! We need to assemble everyone as quickly as possible. Call Marianne Spencer, Don Preston, Patrick Allen and Roxanne de la Rue and ask them to get to the Freemason's Arms for seven-thirty.'

17

A light murmur of conversation reverberated around the Freemason's Arms at twenty-five minutes past seven that evening as the assembled souls awaited the arrival of Kempston Hardwick who, as Ellis Flint had expected, arrived at the very moment the grandfather clock in the corner chimed the half-hour gong.

'Ladies and gentlemen, if you'd all quieten down for a moment, please,' Ellis Flint pleaded.

A voice came from the crowd. 'Who killed my husband?' It was Marianne Spencer.

'That's what we hope to settle once and for all, Mrs Spencer,' Hardwick replied. The conversation died down as the front door to the pub swung open and DI Warner and DC Kerrigan entered the pub to whispered words. 'Ah, good evening, officers. Glad you could join us.'

'Now, what's all this about, Hardwick?' asked Warner.

'Quite simply, I intend to reveal the identity of Charlie Sparks's killer.'

'And what makes you think you have the authority to do that, Hardwick? Besides, this isn't some second-rate detective story. This isn't how we do things in real life,' the policeman said.

'I never claimed to have any authority, Inspector Warner. I have, however, managed to piece together the clues and formulate a theory which exceeds anything the police have yet achieved.' DI Warner fell silent. 'Now, a fair few things struck me as rather odd about the chain of events on the night that Charlie Sparks died. Firstly, why were none of the main suspects present at the time of the murder? Quite simply, they didn't need to be. The dastardly deed had, in fact, been carried out much earlier. It was my associate, Ellis Flint, who led me on to the truth.' Ellis Flint was both flattered by the recognition and confused by the term "associate". 'Of course, I should have realised what had happened before Charlie Sparks even died. The signs were all there while he was still alive.'

'For crying out loud, man!' yelled the voice of Patrick

Allen. 'Are you going to tell us what the hell you think happened, or what?'

'In good time, Mr Allen. Patience is a virtue. And the person who killed Charlie Sparks knows all about patience. In fact, the weapon that killed Charlie Sparks was in place at least some days before he died.'

'Weapon? I thought the police said he was poisoned?' asked Roxanne de la Rue.

'He was. That's about the only thing our esteemed local police force managed to get right.'

The officers began to shuffle their feet and clear their throats.

'Poison is indeed a weapon, Miss de la Rue. It was the way it was conducted which surprised me. No, his food wasn't poisoned by his wife, nor was his drink spiked by an accomplice in the pub that night. When Ellis and I were speaking with Charlie Sparks backstage that night, shortly before his death, he was signing photographs for fans. Do you recall, Ellis?'

'Well yes, I do remember, but what does that have to do with—'

'Don't you remember what he said? He made some remark about how revoltingly bitter the postage stamps and envelopes tasted nowadays!'

'What on earth does that—'

'Bitter, Ellis! Bitter! Postage stamps and envelopes aren't bitter! Strychnine, however, is!'

'Strychnine? You mean to say...'

'Yes! Charlie Sparks was poisoned by the postage stamps!'

'But who—'

'I believe, quite firmly, that Charlie Sparks was poisoned by the very person with whom his wife, Marianne Spencer, was having an affair.'

The room fell into a hushed silence as the heads began to turn and look at Marianne Spencer and, most importantly, Patrick Allen.

'I knew it!' Roxanne de la Rue exclaimed. 'You wanted him out of the way so you could carry on with your sordid affair!'

'How dare you!' Marianne Spencer shouted back. 'Who the hell are you to speak about marriage and sexual morals?'

'Ladies, please. As I said, I believe Charlie Sparks was killed by his wife's lover. When he was signing those photographs, he quite clearly said that he hadn't had to package the envelopes himself for some years, but that he had been left to do them himself. By you, Mr Preston.' Kempston Hardwick glared at Don Preston, who looked nervously from side to side as the eyes of the room fell upon him.

'I beg your pardon! Just what proof do you think you have, exactly?'

'For years, it was you, as his manager, who packaged and sent off the signed photographs, but on the night of his murder you insisted that you didn't have the time to do so, and that Charlie Sparks should do it himself, thereby being slowly poisoned by the heavily strychnine-laced stamps and envelopes. Now, it stands to reason that you would profit immensely from the death of your client. I should imagine DVD sales would soar, wouldn't you say?' He gave Don Preston no time to reply. 'But that's not all, is it? It wasn't Patrick Allen who had been conducting an affair with Marianne Spencer at all. It was you.'

'Well! I've never heard such nonsense in all my life! And just how do you think I got hold of bloody strychnine?'

The eyes of the room fell again on Patrick Allen.

'Well, the obvious line of suspicion falls again on Mr Allen as the beleaguered business partner of Charlie Sparks. The pharmaceuticals business, no less. Oh no, I've no doubt that Wellington Pharmaceuticals was the source of the strychnine.'

'Now, you take that back at once! I've told you, I had nothing to do with this!' Patrick Allen protested.

'I never once claimed that you did, Mr Allen. In

fact,' Hardwick said, as he glanced at his watch, 'I think the matter should be resolved in just a few seconds.'

The crowd looked around at each other, unsure what to make of Hardwick's comments. A few moments later, the door to the Freemason's Arms creaked open and the frame of Billy Reynolds entered the bar.

'Ah-ha, just in time. For those of you who don't already know him, this young man is Billy Reynolds. Of course, some of you may already know him. Perhaps as an employee of Wellington Pharmaceuticals. Or perhaps, Mr Preston, as your step-son.'

A number of audible gasps rang around the room. Don Preston seemed resigned to the unravelling ball of lies.

'You see, you had conducted this whole charade so carefully. Oh, it was well thought out, I'll give you that. A step-son with a different surname who worked at Wellington Pharmaceuticals could easily obtain strychnine without anyone noticing. After all, he was in charge of the accounts and IT records, so who better to fiddle a few numbers? Add to that the probability that suspicion would fall directly onto Patrick Allen, with the possibility of a conviction leading to the business and its assets falling directly into the lap of your lover, Marianne Spencer, and you've got a pretty solid motive. Let's not forget that any in-depth audit of Wellington Pharmaceuticals' accounts would reveal the payments made to Marianne Spencer's company, Net Marketing Solutions – money intended to fund your new life together. Am I somewhere near the truth, Mr Preston?' Don Preston said nothing, and continued to stare at the floor.

'The rest of you need not feel guiltless, though. Although it may have been the poisoned stamps administered by Don Preston which stopped Dave Spencer's heart from beating, it was the web of lies and deceit which killed him. The deceit which led to you, Billy Reynolds, obtaining a deadly poison which you must have at least suspected would be used for no good. The acts through which you, Marianne Spencer, deceived your husband by carrying out an affair with his agent and obtained money through his company. Even you, Miss de la Rue, are not infallible. You knowingly entered into a relationship with a married man. Indeed, this entire sorry saga could be said to originate with that very act. Would Marianne Spencer have begun an affair with Don Preston had she not suspected her husband's own infidelity? Only she can answer that. No, I have no doubt that our esteemed police officers here will find Don Preston guilty of murder and Billy Reynolds of conspiracy to murder, but I don't think any sane man could argue that each and every one of you is, in at least some small way, responsible for the demise and death of

Dave Spencer. It seems that bitterness was the killer in more ways than one.' Hardwick gestured for the two police detectives to begin their procedures and stepped down from the stage to stunned silence. It was Ellis Flint who spoke first to Hardwick.

'I suppose you're right. Everyone had their part to play in the death of Charlie Sparks, be it deliberate or not.'

'Indeed,' replied Hardwick. 'All too often we make decisions and carry out actions without any regard whatsoever for the consequences.'

'So what now?'

'Now? Now it's time for us to take a back seat. The situation will resolve itself, as all situations inevitably do. No, I don't imagine Marianne Spencer will carry on with Don Preston for much longer. You surely must have seen the look in her eyes when she realised her lover had killed her husband. As much as a woman scorned can appear not to care, it was plain from the start that Marianne Spencer still loved her husband very much. It's bitter-sweet that the victim's financial complications will quite probably be resolved by his death. It's the unfortunate but familiar paradox that any artist will be infinitely more successful in death than in life.'

'But surely all of his money will go to Roxanne de la Rue?'

'Not so, it seems. The will which we found in his house was never actually filed with a solicitor. I have one or two friends in the bar and one of them confirmed that Dave Spencer's entire estate was to be left to Marianne. It seems, perhaps, that the victim may have been playing his own game in leading us and, perhaps more pertinently, Marianne into believing that she would not stand to gain in the event of his death.'

'But why?' Ellis Flint asked.

'Who knows? Perhaps he wanted to cause her some temporary anguish. The important point is that it was only ever to be temporary. Only in death would his true feelings and values be apparent. I don't pretend to know all there is to know about human behaviour, Ellis. Detection is a work of instinct and deduction over all else. Human emotion is of very little interest to me.'

Ellis Flint nodded, unsure of quite what to say in return. 'Well, another drink, then?'

'I think that would be just the ticket, Ellis.'

'Campari?'

'Oh, no. I think I need something a little less bitter.'

GET MORE OF MY BOOKS FREE

Thank you for reading *Exit Stage Left*. I hope it was as much fun for you as it was for me writing it.

To say thank you, I'd like to invite you to my exclusive *VIP Club*, and give you some of my books and short stories for FREE. All members of my VIP Club have access to FREE, exclusive books and short stories which aren't available anywhere else.

You'll also get access to all of my new releases at a bargain-basement price before they're available anywhere else. Joining is absolutely FREE and you can leave at any time, no questions asked. To join the club,

head to adamcroft.net/vip-club **and two free books will be sent to you straight away!**

If you enjoyed the book, please do leave a review at the store you bought it from. Reviews mean an awful lot to writers and they help us to find new readers more than almost anything else. It would be very much appreciated.

I love hearing from my readers, too, so please do feel free to get in touch with me. You can contact me via my website, on Twitter @adamcroft and you can 'like' my Facebook page at facebook.com/adamcroftbooks.

For more information, visit my website: adamcroft.net

THE WESTERLEA HOUSE MYSTERY

Hardwick and Flint return in

THE WESTERLEA HOUSE MYSTERY

OUT NOW

When TV psychic Oscar Whitehouse is found murdered inside a locked room, private detective Kempston Hardwick and his friend Ellis Flint are called in to investigate.

Within a matter of days, a second murder takes place in the small village of Tollinghill and a local resident claims she saw the already-dead Oscar Whitehouse at the scene, apparently alive and well. Hardwick and Flint realise they have more than just a conventional mystery on their hands. Can they uncover the secret of the Tollinghill murders, before it's too late?

Turn the page to read the first chapter...

The bowl of sweets clinked and rattled as the long, slender digits plunged in to retrieve a handful of sugar-laced goodness.

'Oh, for Christ's sake!' the man exclaimed, throwing his treasure back into the bowl with a clink and a clatter. 'I specifically said no blue ones!'

The make-up artist peered enquiringly over his shoulder as their eyes met in the mirror.

'Sorry, Mr Whitehouse. It's not really my remit, but I'll go and find the person responsible.'

'No, no. Leave it,' the man replied, his eerie tones reminiscent of Vincent Price, or so she thought. 'Not much point now. I'll be on in five minutes anyway. Honestly, the whole thing has been a shambles. I clearly asked them for Belmore Hills spring water, and they ve me Shaffington Falls! I mean, why should I bother equesting a rider if you're only going to ignore it?'

'Mmmm, I know. Terrible,' the make-up artist responded, her attention focused purely on the dark powder that she was applying to his eyes. Each time she had met him, he had insisted on being made to look eerie, as he had phrased it. She was quite sure that his un-made-up face looked far eerier than anything she could ever muster with her GNVQs and GHDs.

'Three minute call, Mr Whitehouse. We'll be starting in just a mo,' the balding head said as it peered around the half-open door, its face far cheerier than it needed to be.

Oscar Whitehouse instinctively checked his watch. Although he couldn't stand being late for anything, he also had a particular dislike for over-exaggeration.

'Right. I think that's eerie enough, thank you, Charlotte. I'd best be heading through,' he said to the make-up artist.

'Right you are, Mr Whitehouse,' she replied. 'Knock 'em dead!'

He paused briefly. 'Oh, I'll be doing far more than that, don't you worry.'

He squinted under the bright lights as the black-shirted production staff led him through the darkened wings before asking him to wait at the final door. The speech from inside the studio was now more than audible.

'So please give a very warm welcome to my guest, Oscar Whitehouse!'

The green lighting effects and creaking door noise, courtesy of the sound department, would have had Oscar Whitehouse convulsing at the sheer galloping insolence were it not for the camera now trained on his face. Turning to feign laughter at what he knew he must accept as absolutely hilarious, he raised his hand in a casual wave to the audience, shook the host's hand and sat down on the sofa.

'Good afternoon, Oscar. Did you like the welcome?' the bright orange host asked, his teeth gleaming like two rows of ivory soldiers.

'Oh, yes, absolutely. Very good indeed,' he replied, the blood now seeping from his heavily-bitten tongue. 'Very original.'

'Now, Oscar, you're known all over the country and, indeed, all over the world for your paranormal investigations and insight into the supernatural. What was it that first had you interested in the supernatural realm?'

Never been asked that one before, he thought to himself, before replying, graciously. 'Well, I remember one particular experience back when I was a young boy,' he said, before pausing for dramatic effect. 'I was lying in

one night – I must have only been six or seven years
ld – and I recall having the overriding urge to sit bolt
upright. When I did, I saw my grandmother standing at
the end of my bed, telling me everything was going to be
all right. When I woke up the next morning, my father
told me that my grandmother had died in the night, at
the exact time I saw her in my bedroom.'

The on-cue oohs and aahs from the audience were
perfectly timed as Oscar Whitehouse reeled out the
story for the hundredth time. He was always amazed
that the press hadn't yet discovered that his grandmother
was actually alive and well in a nursing home in Bognor
Regis. (If 'well' could be used to describe a woman who
dribbled constantly and was convinced that Richard
Madeley was the devil incarnate.) Seven television sets
later, the family had wisely decided that she'd be far
better off with a radio, following which, she had taken up
the notion that the Shipping Forecast was actually a
daily dose of Nazi propaganda.

The interview carried on in its inane manner, and
Oscar Whitehouse continued to discuss his new book,
Life After Death: A History of Supernatural Activity in
the Afterlife, in a thinly-veiled manner only ever seen on
daytime television.

'Now, you've been on our screens for a few years,
and have taken part in hundreds, if not thousands of

paranormal investigations,' the host continued, shifting to cross his legs the other way for the umpteenth time that minute. 'And your book focuses almost solely on your belief that our spirits live on after death. Do you expect that this book will convince the nay-sayers that the paranormal world is real?'

Oscar Whitehouse chuckled as he rubbed at his fingernail. 'No, I expect there will always be cynics. However, I know that the world will soon have proof of life after death. That much is true. Evil will always live on.'

The oohs and aahs from the audience were well cued by the school-leaver in the black t-shirt, who flailed his arms at the front when wishing to elucidate any sort of audience reaction. A nervous chuckle from the host ensured that the interview moved on rather swiftly, and he turned to address camera five.

'Oscar Whitehouse, for the moment, thank you. Now,' the host began his sentence in his well-accustomed way. 'We're on the lookout for haunted houses all over the country for a new feature on this programme. Do you live in, or know of, a haunted house anywhere in Britain? Perhaps your house – or your friend's house – has its very own spooky spectre. If so, give us a call and we'll get you on for a chat later in the show.'

The host stood from his interview chair and made

his way over to the maniacally-grinning potters whose whirring machinery graced the other side of the stage, ready and waiting for the next ten soul-destroying minutes of television.

* * *

Ellis Flint used to quite like Greensleeves. But, having been kept on hold for an interminable amount of time listening to the piece, he had seriously considered forgetting all about his reason for calling and instead subjecting the other party to an historical diatribe on how Henry VIII had tried (and, with hindsight, hilariously failed) to claim that he had written it. When the phone was finally answered, he decided that plan of action would be a little too heavy for a Friday afternoon, and instead reverted to his initial script.

'Oh, yes, hello there. I'm just calling about the piece you're doing on haunted houses. It's about a friend of mine, actually, who lives in a really spooky old house at Tollinghill. Used to be a rectory. The place gives me the creeps.'

The over-excitement of the production assistant on the other end of the phone seemed to indicate that take-up for this particular segment of the show had been disappointing at best. As a result, Ellis Flint was very quickly assured that he would be put through to the host in the next few moments.

Ellis smiled and sat back down to enjoy the rest of the programme.

Want to read on?

Visit   adamcroft.net/book/the-westerlea-house-mystery/ to grab your copy.

murders in Mildenheath. The complete truth, however, is a little too close for comfort...

For more information, visit my website: adamcroft.net